CAMEL BELLS

JANNE CARLSSON

CAMEL BELLS

Translated by Angela Barnett-Lindberg

A GROUNDWOOD BOOK
DOUGLAS & McINTYRE
TORONTO VANCOUVER BERKELEY

Groundwood Books / Douglas & McIntyre
720 Bathurst Street, Suite 500, Toronto, Ontario M5S 2R4

Distributed in the USA by Publishers Group West
1700 Fourth Street, Berkeley, CA 94710

National Library of Canada Cataloging in Publication
Carlsson, Janne
Camel bells / Janne Carlsson ; translated by Angela Barnett-Lindberg
Translation of: Kamelklockorna.
ISBN 0-88899-515-6 (bound).–ISBN 0-88899-516-4 (pbk.)
I. Barnett-Lindberg, Angela II. Title.
PZ7.C22Ca 2002   J839.73'74   C2002-903155-9

Library of Congress Control Number: 2002109003

Cover illustration by Harvey Chan
Design by Michael Solomon
Printed and bound in Canada

Fo

and their mother

Historical Note

In September 2001, terrorist attacks in the United States triggered a war in Afghanistan, a country of mountains and deserts in central Asia. But this war is just the latest in a series of struggles that have torn apart the country for more than twenty years. *Camel Bells* is set at the beginning of this period, in the late 1970s.

In the summer of 1978, a left-wing group, supported by what was then the Soviet Union, took over Kabul, the capital city of Afghanistan. Many people, like Mir and Anvar, hoped this would mark the change from a corrupt central government to a fairer system that would benefit the poor and illiterate. But the new government was plagued with troubles and, in December 1979, thousands of Soviet troops invaded Afghanistan, claiming to come to the aid of the government and bringing tanks and artillery.

There was resistance to the Soviet invasion, and pockets of rebels, called mujahidin, sprang up all over the country. The resistance grew when living conditions became worse and worse, and Afghans realized that their villages and crops were being destroyed in the Soviet attempt to control the rebels.

Frontier mountain settlements like Hajdar's were among the hardest hit. The Soviets bombed villages and farms in an attempt to close escape routes and prevent the locals from giving food and shelter to the mujahidin. Like Hajdar and his family, millions of Afghans decided to flee their country. Many made their way on foot through the mountain passes that led across the border to sprawling refugee camps in Pakistan. Others fled to Iran.

Even with their helicopters, tanks and thousands of troops, the Soviets found the persistent and scattered pockets of rebels impossible to defeat in the mountainous terrain. Because this was the period of the Cold War between the United States and the Soviet Union, the U.S. supplied the mujahidin with ground-to-air missiles that were effective against enemy helicopters, and neighboring Pakistan provided bases where guerrilla groups, like the one Saber joins, could find food and reinforcements. Fighters came from all over the Muslim world to support their Islamic brothers in their fight against the Soviet Union.

Realizing it was involved in a war it could not win, the Soviets withdrew from Afghanistan in 1989. But the conflict did not end, as different armed groups within the country fought for power. In 1996, the Taliban army, one of the former mujahidin militias, took control of Kabul and moved on to take over most of the country. Some of the fighters from the Arab world who had helped the mujahidin came back to support the Taliban. Among them were Osama bin Laden and his al-Qaeda group.

The U.S.-led invasion that began in the fall of 2001 forced the Taliban from power in Kabul. A new interim government is in place, but its control of the country as a whole is shaky, as power struggles erupt between the very same groups that originally fought the Soviets, and foreign armies from countries like the United States, Canada and Britain continue to occupy the country.

Meanwhile, the people of Afghanistan face the enormous task of rebuilding a country devastated by more than two decades of war.

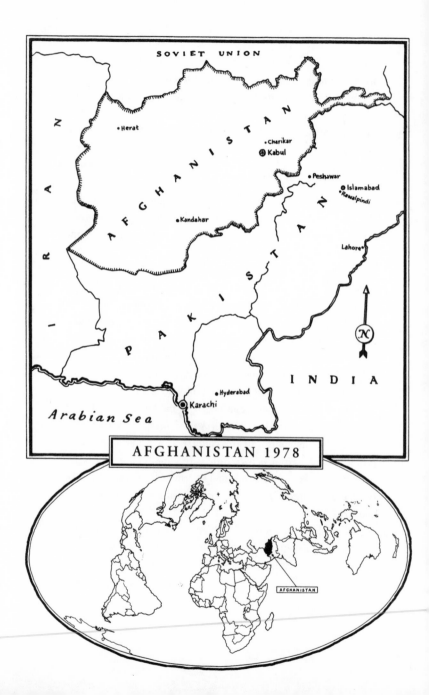

AFGHANISTAN 1978

1

IT was almost pitchdark now. Hajdar could only see a few steps in front of him, but still he stubbornly continued up the narrow path. He heard his mother's heavy breathing as she tried to keep up with him. He couldn't hear his sister, Fatima, but he knew that she was struggling along a little farther behind.

Hajdar gritted his teeth and tried not to think about the snakes and scorpions that might be lying in wait in the dark. His feet hurt. His broken sandals were no longer much good at protecting his feet from the sharp stones and prickly bushes, and he knew the laces on his shoes would not last much longer. If it wasn't so dark, he could at least avoid the sharpest stones, but right now his feet just trod on anything. The pain almost made him scream out when he landed on the sharp desert thorns.

He began to wonder if he had done the right thing. Would his sister and his mother, Bibigoll, have the strength to go on another day? When they had set off, their bundle of dark flatbread seemed so large and heavy that Fatima laughed and said she had not seen so much bread since the last wedding in their

Afghanistan village. She was no longer laughing. Now there were only a few hard crusts left.

They had eaten a lot of it themselves, and Bibigoll had insisted on sharing the bread with hungry travelers they had met on the way. Hajdar sighed. Weren't they in more need themselves? Did they really help anyone by starving to death out here in the wilderness?

His stomach was screaming for bread, rice, eggs fried in lots of fat, yoghurt. He forced himself to think of something else. His thirst was, in fact, worse than his hunger. Bibigoll was carrying the brown water jug over her shoulder. There were still a few mouthfuls left, but they did not dare drink any just now. Who knew when they would find more?

"Hajdar," Bibigoll panted. "Hajdar, how much farther do you think we should go tonight?"

"A bit farther," he answered, and tried to make his voice sound firm. He wondered when they would find somewhere to sleep. Would they starve to death first on this mountain path, or die of thirst? Or would they stumble in the dark and disappear down the side of the precipice? He wished he could admit to Fatima and his mother that he no longer had any real idea of where they were heading, but he did not want to frighten them. After all, they only had him to depend on.

Suddenly it felt colder, as the evening winds swept down the mountain. Hajdar pulled his jacket more tightly around him and pulled the strap harder over his shoulder. Although the bundle of bread that Fatima carried had become lighter each day, their load seemed to become heavier. Some blankets and a couple of cooking pots could hardly weigh so much. Hajdar thought about the water-carriers in town who dragged their dripping leather sacks uphill and downhill. Or the hasars who pulled their heavy carts through the narrow alleys of the bazaar. Was this what it felt like?

He remembered his friend Saber once telling him something about high mountains and thin air. Saber had said that things became twice as heavy up at snow level. At the time, Hajdar had thought this was just another of Saber's wild stories. But maybe he was right.

Saber… Hajdar felt his heart ache. Where was he now? Would they ever see each other again?

Hajdar jumped. The noise he heard made him forget how hungry and thirsty he was and how much his feet ached. The noise came nearer, magnified by the echoes between the mountains.

A reconnaissance helicopter! Without thinking, he threw himself flat on the ground. He felt Bibigoll's hands spasmodically gripping his feet. Now he was grateful for the dark. In daylight they would have no chance to remain hidden.

The engine noise sounded louder. It hurt Hajdar's ears. Then the noise disappeared as fast as it had come. They saw a flashing light vanish over the mountain, and everything became quiet.

The grip around Hajdar's feet was released. "The water jug!" Bibigoll sobbed. "When I threw myself to the ground, it broke."

Hajdar couldn't speak. It was Fatima who managed to break the silence. "We'll find new water soon, I'm sure of it, Mother."

Hajdar knew that none of them were convinced. Even if they did find water, how would they carry it? Why hadn't he bought that large plastic bottle he had seen in the bazaar a few weeks ago? Then it had seemed too expensive, but what use now was the extra money that he had hidden in his belt?

Silently, Hajdar stood up and stretched out his hand to Bibigoll. She choked back her sobs and stood up resolutely.

"Come, let's keep going for a bit," he said.

The wind had died down slightly, but it was still cold. It was going to turn into a cold, clear night. Hajdar had a dizzy feeling that they were climbing right up into the stars. On a night like this, he thought, if one stood on a mountain top and stretched up high, it would surely be possible to pull down one of the nearest stars. Then you could sell it in the bazaar and buy anything you wanted with the money. Some sheep. A horse. Or even a bicycle. No one at home in the village had a bicycle. They cost too much money. Besides, what was the point of a bicycle when one could only walk on the mountain paths?

A howling sound could be heard a long way off. Hajdar shivered. Saber had told him that wolves loved human flesh more than anything. Hajdar felt in his belt for his dagger. It had been his father's. Until now he had only kept it in his belt to prove how grownup he was. Many of his friends had looked jealously at the sharp dagger with its long blade. "Made in Charikar," he would say proudly as he let his hand caress the glimmering steel edge. Charikar, the town of the long knives.

The crowd of boys had always sighed in amazement. No one had known anything like it – an eleven-year-old with his own Charikar dagger. At the time Hajdar had always sensed something frightening about the dagger. The blade felt cold and lifeless, and the edge was razor sharp. One could cut open a pomegranate or peel an orange with it, whittle a sallow pipe, or cut through the thickest rope in a flash. But Hajdar knew that was not why the knifemaker had forged the dagger.

His thoughts went back to the festival of Gorban – the happiest day of the year. On Gorban, no one worked, and everyone ate the finest food, drank masses of tea, visited each other and dressed up in their best. Meat was saved for the poor, so that on this day even the beggars could be happy.

One year on Gorban, Saber and Hajdar had been

walking along the village road in their best clothes. They had hardly dared play for fear of dirtying their white trousers. Hajdar's long white tunic had been heavily embroidered by his grandmother, who had spent hours sewing each stitch.

The festivities had hardly begun when it happened. Hajdar's father walked out onto the village road. He was carrying the dagger in his hand and drying it off on the inside of his embroidered vest. There was blood on the knife, on Father's hands and in the dust on the road.

After that, Hajdar couldn't stop thinking about the dagger. All at once he realized why there was so much mutton at Gorban time. He had known that many sheep were sacrificed, but it was not until then that he really understood what slaughter meant. The bloody dagger. His father's bloody hands. Drops of blood on the dusty road. When he was given the dagger some years later, he hoped desperately that he would never need to use it as a slaughtering knife.

Now when Hajdar took a firmer grip on the knife he wondered if he might have to use it on the wolf tonight.

The burden on his back began to feel unbearably heavy again. Would they never reach the ridge of the hill? During the day when they followed the twisting path along the cliff edge, it seemed so many times as though they would soon reach the highest point of their climb. But every time they reached a ledge, the path stubbornly continued to new heights. Several times Fatima looked as though she would start crying with disappointment. Then she clenched her teeth, and after a few minutes' rest they continued. Mother refused to eat anything the whole day. She said that she didn't feel hungry, but both Fatima and Hajdar knew that she wasn't eating anything for their sakes. They tried to coax her to take some of the hard bread bits in Fatima's bundle.

"Just up the next ridge," thought Hajdar out loud. "Then we'll rest a while." He noticed that he was whispering. He didn't know why, but Grandmother used to say that walls have rats and rats have ears, and that was just how he felt about the dark. Even though on one side the mountain descended sharply into the abyss, and on the other side was only the mountain, it felt as though a hundred enemies were lying in wait behind every corner.

"I don't think I have any more strength, Hajdar." For the first time Bibigoll said what the children had been afraid of hearing. Hajdar was ashamed that his mother had eaten nothing all day.

He took her hand. It frightened him to feel how cold and sweaty it was. "Lean against me. Perhaps we can find somewhere to rest a little higher up," he said, though he knew there was only a small chance of this.

As they struggled along the narrow cliff shelf, Hajdar's legs became numb with tiredness. He felt as if he was watching himself from a distance. It occurred to him that Saber would have laughed at the sight of the three of them staggering along, and for a few seconds, Hajdar couldn't help smiling. Faster than expected they dragged themselves up to the next ledge.

It was Fatima who noticed it first.

"Look, a broad ledge. Maybe we can sleep here."

Even if Hajdar didn't like the fact that she had discovered it before him, he had to agree with her. Really they should continue until they found water, and they had to find better protection before daylight. Now that they were so close to the Pakistan border, they couldn't continue once it was light. He thought of the wolves and how dangerous cold could be. But his body screamed for rest.

"We'll rest here a while," he said. In a few seconds he released himself from the heavy packing, undid the straps and rolled out the blankets. He hurried a little too much and a pot rolled away in the dark with a clatter.

Fatima spread a thin blanket over the stony path. She pulled it as close to the mountain wall as possible so that no one would be too near the sharp precipice on the other side of the ledge. They shared the other two blankets and crept close together to keep warm.

Hajdar looked up at the stars, which seemed closer than ever. Mother and Fatima were asleep already, exhausted and breathing heavily. Far away he could hear a wolf howling.

2

TWO years before Hajdar began his long walk with Fatima and Mother, spring came to their village. The hills, which were dried by the sun for most of the year, were green and luxuriant. Below the bare mountain the ground shone red with poppies and wild tulips.

The kotschis, or nomads, would travel in long caravans over the plains, looking for grazing ground. Wherever the ground was green, they would set up camp with their large, black-brown cloth tents. In the winter they would disappear down the plains, and in the summer they would move higher up the mountains to find green pasture for their sheep and camels. On quiet spring nights Hajdar could hear the camel bells of the caravans tinkling in the distance.

Saber had wild stories to tell of how the kotschis kidnapped children from the villages or stole gold from the rich after cutting their throats. Hajdar didn't know how much was true. But he always felt something eerily tempting when he lay there on his mattress on the clay floor and heard the tinkling noise somewhere far away. He wished he could go with the nomads one summer, to learn their strange language and see the world on the other side of the mountain.

On that spring day, ten-year-old Hajdar was walking along the winding village path. It was Nau Roz, the Afghan new year, and the stream that flowed outside the village was full. The melted water from the mountain was too cold to swim in, but Saber and some of the village boys were jumping in anyway. Hajdar laughed at their terrified expressions as they hit the ice-cold water.

When Saber caught sight of Hajdar, he waved. With one leap he was up on the beach, and before Hajdar knew what was happening, Saber had given him a hug and shouted, "Happy New Year." Hajdar drew back quickly, but the front of his tunic was soaking wet. The boys around them had a good laugh, and Hajdar soon joined in. He couldn't be cross with Saber for very long. His friend's smile nearly reached up to his oversized ears.

"Why don't you come to my place for a while?" Saber said to Hajdar.

"Sure." Hajdar was pleased that Saber was inviting just him. Saber was at least thirteen years old, but he looked older. No one could believe that there was only three years' difference between him and skinny, little Hajdar. If he could be a friend of Saber's, then he didn't mind being teased sometimes.

The boys walked around the village, where water

from the stream led into many small irrigation channels that surrounded the small fields.

At this time of year there was plenty of water. But it was different in the summer when the stream almost dried out. Then the farmers had to take turns using the water for a few hours each. Sometimes a farmer would let water from a neighbor's field into his own plot of land. Saber knew many stories of people who had even killed each other for the sake of water.

Villages farther away on the plain, where the stream's water didn't reach, got water through long, underground tunnels that stretched for miles. When the underground tunnels collapsed, the land turned back to desert, and the villages would be abandoned. Sometimes the people who laid the tunnels were buried alive right down there under the ground.

"Welcome, welcome," said Saber loudly with an exaggerated bow when they arrived at his house a little later. He opened the door in the mud wall and ushered Hajdar into the little yard.

Saber had six younger brothers and sisters, all under ten years of age. When they noticed Hajdar, they made a beeline for him. Hajdar liked Saber's family. He only had Fatima, who was a few years older than himself. Bibigoll had almost died when Hajdar was born, so she couldn't have any more children, however much Hajdar longed for them. Their family was the smallest in the village. Everyone was sorry for Hajdar's father because he only had one son.

Hajdar let all of Saber's little brothers and sisters form a ring around him. He pretended to be a wolf and bit first one, then the other. The small children screamed with laughter.

"Salam, Hajdar!" It was Saber's father. Hajdar, a little embarrassed, immediately stopped playing wolf. "Happy New Year," Saber's father continued. "It's good to see you. Come in and have some tea!"

In a corner of the yard, smoke was coming out of a chimney from the little hut where Saber's mother was baking the day's bread. Her face was flushed from the heat, and she was bent over the oven in the floor. Dough was rising in a large trough nearby. She formed a huge flat, rectangular cake and flattened it onto a wet baker's peel. Then she quickly bent over the hot hole of the oven and attached the bread to its inner wall. If the bread was placed too hard against the oven wall, it would burn and one could never get it off. If it was placed too gently, it would fall down among the hot embers and burn.

Saber's mother already had a dozen steaming baked loaves rolled up in a piece of cloth in a basket.

"Take this basket in," she said to Saber. "I'll come with the rest when I've finished baking."

When they were inside, Saber began to boil water in the open fireplace. It wasn't long before both he and Hajdar each had a pot of tea in front of them on the floor. They leaned back on the mattresses that were arranged along the walls. Saber fetched sugar, raisins, apricot pips and dried mulberry figs from a cupboard.

"Did you know that dried raisins grow on trees on the other side of the mountain?" Saber said earnestly, his eyes wide. "They are as large as oranges and much sweeter than these raisins. If you eat one of those, you feel full for several days."

"Can you bring some the next time you go there so that I can taste one?" asked Hajdar.

"The raisin king would never agree to that. You are allowed to pick up the giant raisins where they hang in clusters on the tree," Saber went on. "But anyone who tries to take some away is punished. I tried to take a raisin away in my pocket once, but it stuck out a bit and the guards saw it. If I hadn't been a friend of the raisin king's daughter, I would certainly have been beheaded. They have already beheaded several hundred raisin thieves. No, I'm certainly not going to try that again."

"You're a friend of the raisin king's daughter?" Hajdar said suspiciously.

"Oh, yes," Saber answered. "She's going to marry the king of Kabul, you know."

"What? He's so old. Besides, he doesn't even live in Afghanistan anymore."

"That's what you think. I saw him and the raisin king's daughter in a tea house in Kabul when I was there last. They sat there eating giant raisins and drinking tea. The raisin king's daughter smiled sweetly at me every time the old king looked the other way."

Hajdar decided it was time to change the subject. He slurped his warm tea loudly and asked, "When are you going to Kabul next?"

"In a few days. I'm going to stay with Mir for a whole week."

Mir was Saber's uncle. He was the only one in the family who had gone to high school. He had worked for a year as a construction worker in Iran and saved quite a bit of money. Now he was employed in a bank in Kabul. Mir liked to receive visitors from the village, and Saber had been to Kabul a few times with his father. When he returned to the village he told Hajdar the strangest stories. Hajdar knew that some of them were probably just Saber's normal wild tales, but still, Kabul sounded like a wonderful place. Hajdar had often dreamed of going there with Saber, but he knew his mother was terrified at the thought. Who knew what dangers there were in the large city? Wicked people and scoundrels. Cars that ran you down. Bazaars where young boys might get lost. And crowds everywhere. Hajdar was certainly not going into that confusion, no matter how much he nagged. Besides, they could always ask the neighbors to bring back material and thread and medicine during their trips to Kabul, and they could get everything else in the village.

But Hajdar dreamed of seeing the world beyond the other side of the mountain, especially when he listened to the bells of the nomads' camels in the dusk.

"Mir thinks that I should take as many raisins as I can carry," Saber was saying. "He says you can sell them in the bazaar for a lot of money. Last year's harvest is almost gone in Kabul now. One can even sell flowers. Mir says foreigners will pay ten or even twenty afghanis for a bouquet of wild tulips. Father didn't think I could manage at first, but now he thinks it's a good idea. Right now he has a lot to do with the farm and the cattle, so this time I shall go alone."

"Aren't you scared?" asked Hajdar carefully.

For the first time Saber looked a little uncertain. "It'll be fine," he said slowly. "Though if you could come with me, it would be even better."

Hajdar couldn't believe his ears. Go with Saber to Kabul? For a whole week?

He didn't want to seem too enthusiastic, but soon he and Saber were sitting imagining all the exciting things they would do together. But who could make his mother change her mind? Saber's father thought it would be better if his son didn't go to Kabul alone. When Hajdar had dinner with Saber's family a little later, Saber's father promised to have a word with his mother. This could, after all, bring welcome extra income for Hajdar's family.

Dusk was already beginning to fall when Hajdar

left Saber's house. Instead of going directly home, he took the path around the other side of the village, past the low mud hut opposite the mosque, where he had gone to school for a few years. He had learned to read, write and count. Most of the villages didn't have a school at all, so he had something to be pleased about.

Hajdar had even taught Fatima to read a bit. Bibigoll had wondered what use that was for a girl, but Fatima had stubbornly copied the signs that Hajdar taught her. Soon she could write her name and read small tales that Hajdar wrote down on the blackboard. He had to rub it all out many times before he could write down the whole story, because he only had room for four rows at a time on his blackboard.

Hajdar and Fatima had also learned the most important chapters from the Koran by heart in Arabic. It was a language that they didn't understand, but both the Muslim priest – the mullah – and their mother told them it was important to know.

Hajdar kept walking quickly until he came to a field covered with piles of stones. There were many flags flapping in the evening breeze – bits of cloth attached to warped wooden poles.

He still remembered that day some years earlier. The cries and screams. The mullah's muttered prayers. Everything had happened so fast.

His father woke one morning with a stomach

ache. He felt sick the whole day, and by evening he was so exhausted that he couldn't talk. He beckoned Hajdar to him, took the dagger from his belt and, without saying a word, gave it to his only son. Hajdar wanted to thank him, but they just looked deeply into each other's eyes.

Hajdar's father died early the next morning and he was buried before the evening. Hajdar knew exactly which stones marked out his grave.

A warm spring rain began to spray over the burial place. Hajdar thought how different everything had become after that day. Grandmother, Bibigoll, Fatima and he suddenly had no one who could work the fields. His father's two elder brothers had to take that responsibility, but they had families of their own and really weren't in a position to help anyone else.

His mother had been forced to sell the carpets in order to buy seed to sow. The landowner had received a large amount of the meager harvest, and they had soon eaten up the rest. They hardly ever saw the khan who owned the land. He lived in Kabul and every year he sold grain from the villages he owned for hundreds of thousands of afghanis. Grandmother had sold her gold earrings. Though they were managing, things were still a struggle.

Hajdar woke on the cliff ledge with a start. Fatima had nudged him gently in the side.

"We must go on," she whispered. "It will get light

soon." They woke their mother and rolled up their blankets. Hajdar's body ached and the blankets felt heavy. He suddenly remembered how thirsty he was.

He turned to the others. "Come, let's go," he said quietly.

3

SABER'S father had finally managed to convince Bibigoll to let Hajdar accompany Saber to town. Hajdar hardly dared believe it was true and expected her to change her mind at any minute. The last few days before the journey she talked incessantly about all the things Hajdar shouldn't do in town. "Watch out for cars! Don't get into bad company! Keep a close watch on your money so no one steals it! Obey Saber! Don't forget to be grateful and give Mir food and presents!"

Hajdar stowed away as many raisins as he could carry in a large cloth bundle. Saber's raisin bundle was large, too. They also wanted to try to take as many wild tulips as possible.

The sun had not yet risen when Saber and Hajdar met to pick wild tulips. The desert bloomed just on the other side of the village fields, and the tulips were still closed in the darkness. Both boys shivered in the cold morning air. It didn't take them long to pick hundreds of flowers and carefully roll them in wet rags. As they walked back to the village, they could already hear the mullah's slightly hoarse voice calling people to the day's first prayer hour.

At home, Hajdar quickly ate some bread. He hurried so he would not have to see his mother's worried face and listen to her advice.

Then, with their bundles of tulips and raisins tied securely on their backs, they began to follow the twisting path over the fields and hills. As usual, Hajdar found it a little difficult to keep up with Saber. He felt as though he had to keep trotting along while Saber walked with long, even strides.

Slightly puffed, they came out to the main road. Several minibuses drove past without taking the slightest notice of the two boys. Then a red minibus approached, and the boys waved eagerly. The brakes screeched and soon they were on board with their bundles. There were no seats left, so they had to stand right at the front behind the driver. The driver played loud music on a cassette deck while he sat marking the beat on the steering wheel. He turned to Hajdar and Saber with a broad smile.

"Where are you going, boys?"

"To Kabul," Saber shouted in his ear.

"What are you going to do there?" He had to shout as loudly as he could to drown out the noise of the engine and the cassette.

"Say hello to my uncle," yelled Saber.

"What have you got in the bundles, then?"

"Raisins."

"But I'm sure you haven't got raisins in that wet bundle?"

Hajdar looked admiringly at the driver, who seemed able to steer the bus without looking at the road. What an art! Especially on the twisting mountain pass they had come to. He plucked up his courage and answered before Saber had a chance.

"No, those are flowers."

"And what's the name of the lady who's going to get those?" teased the driver. Then he laughed and began to sing along with the cassette music in a squeaky voice. Some men behind Hajdar and Saber had heard the conversation and were having a good laugh. One of them had five hens with their legs tied together on his lap. From time to time they cackled, but generally they seemed quite content. The men passed around a rusty tin that was soon full of green tobacco that they had spat out.

Tired, hungry babies in the back of the bus screamed until their mothers lifted their veils and let them breastfeed. Apart from this, the din inside the bus became worse and worse. Everyone had to shout at each other in order to be heard, and the noise grew louder as they all shouted more and more.

The old man with the hens nudged the boys and offered them salted roasted peas. They took a fistful each. The old man was leaning over Saber to offer the bus driver some, too, when suddenly the bus careened to one side. The brakes screeched, people screamed, and all five chickens cackled at once. The bus stopped with a shuddering jolt, and the old man with the roasted peas was left hanging over Saber. It began to rain peas as the bag he had been holding rolled away.

The bus driver swore and shook his fist angrily at someone outside. In the middle of the road in front of the bus swarmed sheep, camels and beautifully dressed nomads. They had appeared from nowhere as the bus had gone around a bend at full speed. In order not to crash into a camel, the bus had swerved away and was now on the wrong side of the road. As quick as a flash, the bus driver turned off his cassette machine and opened his window. Now it was completely silent in the bus. Even the hens were quiet. Hajdar suddenly thought of all the terrible stories he had heard about nomads – about their long knives and their habit of fighting. He tried not to think about the dagger in his belt.

Some of the nomads' dogs angrily rushed toward the bus. The driver just had time to slam his window shut before the dogs threw themselves at the side of the bus and snarled at the window panes.

Hajdar couldn't take his eyes off the drooling mouths of the dogs. The dogs of the nomads did not have ears and tails. They had these removed as newborn puppies and were then made to suck the blood from their own cut-off ears. People said that was why they were so bloodthirsty.

When the passengers got over their fright, they began to shout suggestions to the driver. Some thought he should drive away as quickly as possible. Others advised him to stick a knife in the dogs. He began to look thoroughly confused. Now sheep and camels were all around the bus. One camel parked itself right in front of the windscreen and turned its behind to them.

Beyond the herds of sheep, a large, gaily painted truck approached from the other direction. Even from this distance Hajdar could read the large green letters above the driver's cabin. "God protect us," it said in Arabic. The truck driver hooted angrily, but the sheep pretended not to notice him.

Now one of the nomads began to move between the animals toward the bus. He was tall, well built and had a black turban and a brightly colored waist-coat over a bright blue tunic and trousers. His clothes flapped in the wind. Hajdar avoided the nomad's penetrating eyes as the man approached the bus window and gestured to the driver to open it.

The driver drew the window aside a little uncertainly, and the two men began talking to each other in a language Hajdar did not understand. In his village everyone spoke Dari, but this language must be Pashto — the same language he sometimes heard on the radio at Saber's, and which the nomads spoke to each other as they went past on the plain outside Hajdar's village.

At first both the tall man and the bus driver made a mass of angry movements with their arms and hands. They looked grim. Then the movements became a little gentler, and Hajdar could see something that resembled a smile on the nomad's lips. The bus driver wiped the sweat from his brow, and his bearded face no longer looked so tense. He turned the ignition key and began to creep forward very slowly, while the black-turbaned man waved to some small boys who ran in front of the bus and drove the sheep away. Their heavy fat tails bounced up and down as the boys whistled and shouted and beat them with their sticks. On the other side of the sheep the colorful truck was waiting impatiently. Already another bus and two cars were behind him. They honked from time to time, but to no avail.

Hajdar looked a little enviously at the nomad boys. He wondered what it would be like to be able to travel with them, learn their language and see everything that they could see. He almost forgot that he was already on the greatest adventure of his life.

Hajdar had often dreamed about going to Kabul. That was where the radio programs came from. That was where people were rich, happy and carefree. Being a farmer, on the other hand, was a hard life. One never knew if the food would last to the next harvest. Since his father had died, Hajdar understood even more how hard it was to provide food for a whole family — even if it was only a small family.

Finally they came through the sheep flock. The nomad boys waved goodbye, and soon the bus gathered speed. The music was as loud as ever, as the engine strained up the steep hills. From time to time the bus stopped to pick up people waiting by the road.

The bus began to fill up so much that some passengers began to complain, but the driver continued to stop and pick up more and more along the way. The last people had to find room on the roof rack on top of the baggage.

Now the bus was completely full. The engine sounded even more strained as it dragged its heavy load uphill. The bus crawled forward, and several times it had coughing fits like the ones Hajdar's grandmother had at home in the village sometimes.

Hajdar saw the road coiling up the mountain from his window. Sometimes they met trucks and buses that came whizzing down the hills at a frightening speed. More than once Hajdar thought that his last moment had come, and several times he shut his eyes in fear.

The driver turned around and pointed to something at the side of the road. A badly smashed-up truck lay at the bottom of the precipice. Hajdar did not want to think that it might be their turn next. The driver let go of the wheel and held up six fingers to show how many people had died. Then he passed his hand across his neck and shut his eyes for a few seconds. While he did this, the bus swung out a bit just as they were about to go around a bend. An enormous red truck, completely covered with floral paintings, came careening right at them. The bus driver just had time to swing aside before the truck whistled by so close that they nearly touched it. Hajdar and Saber thumped the driver on the back and they laughed together in relief, though no one else on the bus seemed to have noticed what had happened.

Now the engine was no longer sputtering, but the brakes squealed every time the bus cornered sharply. To Hajdar, who was used to walking or, at best, riding a donkey, it felt wonderful to rush along so quickly.

A little later they came to a couple of mud huts by the side of the road.

"Tea," said the bus driver loudly as he drew up abruptly.

"Isn't it better to keep on driving, so that we can get there sooner?" whined a skinny little man from the back of the bus.

"I have driven all the way from Kandahar, and both the bus and I need a rest," said the driver. The old bus hissed quietly in agreement. Steam came from the engine. "You can see for yourself. It's boiling over."

While everyone got off the bus, the driver fetched water from a nearby well and emptied it over the engine. After a while he was able to take off the radiator lid and fill it with fresh water.

"Well, boys," he said, turning to Hajdar and

Saber, "go fetch me a pot of tea. Buy yourselves some with the change!" They came back after a few minutes with the tea pots, glasses and sugar, while the owner of the tea house cast suspicious looks through the door of the mud hut. He was obviously afraid that someone would disappear with his glasses and pots when he wasn't looking.

The driver's name was Abdul Ali and he was from Kandahar. He had been driving between Kandahar and Kabul for fifteen years. Hajdar and Saber squatted in front of him and rested their tired legs.

He told them how he had once bumped into a camel. Another time he had rolled the bus into a ditch to avoid crashing into a truck. Every window in the bus had been broken, but some truck drivers had helped him right the bus again, and he was able to drive it away. Just in front and just behind the place where the accident had taken place, the road had dropped right down into a precipice. He had just missed being killed.

He told them how he had been attacked by bandits in a mountain pass one dark night. All the passengers were forced to get out of the bus while the bandits searched for money, gold and valuables. Abdul Ali himself had to give them his watch. When the bandits had taken what they wanted, they disappeared with their rifles up into the mountain again. It was better to leave expensive articles at home if one was traveling, he told the boys. It wasn't a good idea to travel in the dark, either, but sometimes Abdul Ali was forced to do so.

The more Hajdar listened, the more convinced he was that he did not want to be a farmer or a nomad. He wanted to be a bus driver. One even got paid for driving around. Perhaps he could save some money and one day buy his own bus. Very carefully he asked Abdul Ali how much a bus cost.

"You'll have to wait a few years, my boy," laughed Abdul Ali. Saber smiled, a little embarrassed, as though Hajdar had asked something stupid.

Okay, laugh, thought Hajdar. Maybe you'll still be laughing when I'm making enough money to buy two buses.

As though he had been reading his thoughts, Saber began to tell the story of a poor hasar man in Kabul who carried heavy loads up and down streets in a harness on his back. He worked harder than everyone else and eventually he was able to buy a cart to pull his load. After some time he was able to buy another cart and hire a man to pull it. A couple of years later he succeeded in buying an old truck, and now he owned ten large new trucks that went back and forth between Afghanistan and Europe.

The passengers began to come back from the tea house and stood impatiently outside the bus. Abdul Ali quickly drank his last glass of tea, and soon they were on their way again.

The chickens had revived during the tea break and

were not at all keen to get back into the crowded bus. They did their best to drown out the noise of the engine and music. The bus rolled faster and faster down the steep slopes, while the driver sang happily.

There were more cars on the road. Some were black and white with Taxi signs on their roofs.

"Does that mean we're nearly there?" Hajdar shouted in Saber's ear. Saber nodded.

Now it wasn't just mountain and desert along the roadside. They passed village after village. Green fields lay around the clay walls and clumps of mud huts. They also saw the odd donkey, led or ridden by boys of Hajdar's age.

On the left Hajdar saw the tallest building he had ever seen. Saber saw his surprised expression and shouted into his ear, "That is the big silo the foreigners built. It is full of grain, and they bake a thick bread that you can't break off, but have to cut with a knife."

There were more and more houses along the roadside now, and people swarmed about. In an open area Hajdar saw lots of parked buses.

"Yes, here we are in Kabul, good people," shouted Abdul Ali, as he stopped the bus in the middle of the crowd.

They had arrived.

4

WHEN the bus stopped in Kabul on that spring day almost two years earlier, Hajdar felt quite dizzy. He didn't know which way to turn. Buses and taxis honked and drove around in what seemed like a complete mess. Hasars dragged their heavy carts through the mass of people. A boy of Hajdar's age was selling boiled chickpeas that he had arranged into an elegant pile. Just next to him was another boy selling sliced cold potatoes. Customers would choose one of the colorful sauces to pour over the slices. Walnuts and apricots were being sold a little farther away. The salesmen tried to drown out each other's voices and the honking of the cars.

Hajdar took a firm grip of his bundles. He had heard many stories about people who came to Kabul and lost everything they owned. How could you know who to trust? Saber stood by Abdul Ali's bus, saying goodbye. Abdul Ali hugged him and said that Saber and Hajdar were like his own sons. If they needed his help at any time, he would be there. Then with a happy farewell toot, he started the bus and drove off.

"How do we know where your uncle lives?" asked Hajdar.

"He doesn't live far from Deh Mazang prison, so we can walk," Saber answered.

It was very cloudy so at least they did not have to walk in the sun, but even so, their bundles seemed heavy. Hajdar was glad that Saber knew the way. When they passed between the cars to cross to the sidewalk on the other side of the street, a taxi nearly knocked Hajdar down. The driver blew his horn angrily and thrust his unshaven face out his window. Hajdar heard him shout something about country bumpkins, but his voice was soon drowned out by all the other persistent honking — his taxi was holding up the traffic.

A thin little boy walked by, balancing a tray on his head. There were at least twenty-five flatbreads piled on the tray. He scampered about like a weasel in spite of the heavy load, until a truck honked at him and he leapt away to avoid being run over. One of his plastic slippers was left in the road, together with two breads that had slid off the top of his pile. The boy picked up the breads again before Hajdar had time to blink. On the way to the sidewalk he kissed both breads before carelessly throwing them up onto the top of the pile again. But what about the plastic slipper? The boy stood there, swaying back and forth on the curb. Hajdar knew he was wondering whether he dared to leave the bread on the sidewalk or whether he should try to go out into the traffic again with the tray on his head.

Hajdar handed his bundle to Saber and ran over to the boy. "I can look after the bread for you," he said a little shyly. Without a word, the boy rushed out into the traffic and grabbed his slipper. Breathlessly he thanked Hajdar for his help. He told him that his name was Hadi and that his father had a kebab restaurant farther down the road.

"Come in and eat a kebab! On me," said Hadi.

Hajdar and Saber looked at each other. They were both hungry, even if it was only mid-morning. But was it all right to accept an invitation from a stranger?"

"We have just eaten… " Saber tried to say.

"Don't be silly," said Hadi. "Come on in with me."

Even outside the little restaurant, one could smell the wonderful smell of kebab. A one-eyed man stood fanning the kebab using a plaited fan to keep the embers going. Skewers with necklaces of meat cubes lay on the grill. They had been marinated overnight in yoghurt and garlic before being cooked on the embers. The man who was grilling the kebab brightened when he caught sight of Hadi.

"Are these your guests? What luck that I have some kebab skewers ready," he laughed. In a flash he set out three plastic plates and placed a flatbread on each. He placed two kebab skewers on top of each bread. "Ready, gentlemen," he announced with a deep bow and his right hand on his heart.

Hadi took them to a table at the back of the restaurant. Many of the guests had put their feet up on the chairs. Hajdar knew that, like him, they were used to sitting on the floor, and that their legs ached hanging down from a chair.

While Hadi ran and fetched a large glass of water for them to share, Hajdar and Saber looked contentedly around them. What a start to their time in Kabul – to be invited for kebab in the middle of the morning by a stranger. They sprinkled salt and red pepper on the meat and tucked into the food. Hadi told them that his father had come to Kabul twenty years earlier, but he still preferred the company of country folk. That was why he had put his kebab restaurant near the bus station, where many people coming in from the country would first stop and eat. Hadi made Hajdar and Saber promise to come back, so he could show them the old bazaars in town. When he heard that the boys were going to try to sell flowers, he advised them to go to the street that the foreigners called Chicken Street which, it turned out, was not far from Saber's uncle's bank.

Full of food, Hajdar and Saber began to walk along a wide tree-lined road. They went past shop after shop. Saber said that in the evening they shut the shops by pulling down a metal wall and locking it with a large padlock. All through the night, soldiers in gray uniforms patrolled the streets to make sure no one tried to break into the shops.

Suddenly the boys found themselves in the middle of a crowd of giggling girls, all dressed in black. Hajdar was surprised that they could walk about in the street without their parents and without being in purdah – the veil most women wore to screen themselves from the sight of strangers. But these girls just wore white shawls around their heads. None of them seemed to notice the boys from the country, and they did not look the slightest bit shy. Perhaps it was lucky for Fatima that she did not live in a town and have to go to school with these girls, Hajdar thought.

"At home we boys were not allowed to go to school properly, and here even the girls are allowed to!" he said to Saber.

"Do you think Hadi can go to school just because he lives in Kabul?" Saber said. "He has to work in his father's restaurant all day. It's just the rich people who send their children to school. Uncle Mir has told me what a difficult time he had when he was studying in Kabul. Sometimes he could eat nothing but bread so he would have enough money for paper and books. The place where he lived was so cramped that he used to study under the streetlights at night."

They passed a man dragging a gigantic load of firewood on a cart. Saber told Hajdar that there was a place not far away where they sold firewood, but one had to make sure it was not soaking wet when it was weighed.

Hajdar thought how much people cheated each

other in town. Everything was so much simpler at home in the village.

The boys hurried. They had to sell the flowers as soon as possible. By this time their bundles were beginning to feel really heavy, so they decided they would try to leave the raisins and everything else with Mir at the bank.

A nomad came walking with five camels in a row, his back as straight as an arrow. He took no notice of the cars and buses that had to swerve to avoid colliding with the camels. It looked as though all the world's buses and cars were nothing compared to one single nomad and his proud camels.

Hajdar thought about his grandmother's tales of camel caravans that had gone along the silk route long before she was born. They had gone over mountains and through deserts. The road was littered with both beast and human skeletons, though the loads of silk had rocked on through the deserts to the countries far beyond the mountains.

The boys went past a cinema with large glass doors, before coming to a traffic circle where cars converged from three different directions. When they finally crossed to the other side of the wide street, Hajdar almost felt like stopping and checking that all the bones in his body were unbroken.

When they had gone a bit farther, Saber furtively pointed to the other side of the road. "The prison is behind those shops," he whispered. "Once when I was in town with my father, I went with Mir to visit one of his workmates there. Some money was missing from the bank. Someone had given money to the judge, so he sentenced Mir's friend even though everyone knew he was innocent. Masses of prisoners sat inside there with ragged clothes, begging. They even have to pay for their food. Mir told me that his friend had been quite fat before, but now he was thin and wretched, and he had lost a lot of teeth because the food was so bad. The friend didn't have any relatives in Kabul so he didn't have visitors very often. Probably he's still sitting there shaking the bars, even though he is as innocent as you or I."

Hajdar looked at the wall behind the shops and noticed a guard marching back and forth. He imagined Mir's friend sitting there in his little cell, slowly starving to death.

The boys passed the entrance to the zoo, and soon came to the Kabul River where people were washing their clothes by the shore. Steam was coming from the small containers in which they boiled the laundry water. Colorful clothes lay on the rocks by the shore, spread out to dry in the sun.

The boys had just sat down on the grass to rest for a bit, when *BOOOOOOOM!!!* The ground shook from the explosion and Hajdar, in pure fright, grabbed hold of Saber, who roared with laughter.

"That was the midday cannon," he said.

"What do you mean?"

"Every day at 12 o'clock it fires a salute, so people know what time it is."

Was that anything to make such a fuss about, Hajdar wondered, when one could see the sun and tell the time of day from it, anyway? Would he be able to stand staying in this town a whole week if life was so full of surprises?

5

A T Mir's bank, Hajdar stayed out on the side-walk while Saber went in to find his uncle. But Mir had gone for lunch, so one of his workmates promised to look after the boys' bundles, and they could collect their things when they met Mir after work that evening.

Outside the bank, Hajdar began to feel a bit worried. Twice a guard waved his rifle and told him to move. Hajdar tried to explain that he was waiting for his friend who was in the bank, but the guard said he had his orders and could not let folks sit on the side-walk just like that. Luckily at that moment Saber came down the bank steps and they began walking to Chicken Street.

Chicken Street was exactly as Hadi had described it. It was lined with shops where everything but chicken was sold. There were rows and rows of leather bags, small hand-knotted rugs, woodwork, blue glass from Herat, embroidered suede clothes, colorful cloth bags and Afghan musical instruments. Wide-eyed, Hajdar looked at the shiny silver rings with large streaky green malachite stones in the gold-smith's shop. The whole shop window shone blue from lapis lazuli stones. It seemed strange that there should be such precious things in the ground if one just dug deep enough. Once Saber had said that all of Afghanistan was full of precious stones and metals, but no one had the money to dig them out.

But it was not the shops that surprised Hajdar the most; it was the people. Even though Saber had told him a lot about his trips to Kabul, Hajdar had never imagined that there were so many different types of people.

Many of them looked like him and Saber. Others had blue eyes and light golden hair. There were long-haired young men in worn-out clothes. Hajdar thought they looked poor, and he wondered how they had managed to get to Kabul. In his village there were many poor people, too, but they didn't usually set off on journeys. And then to see all the girls without veils and scarves. Some of them weren't even accompanied by a man. Hajdar wondered why their fathers let them travel on their own. They laughed and talked loudly with each other in a strange language.

Other foreigners came in large cars and stopped right in front of the places where they wanted to shop. The men were dressed in suits and ties. Their wives wore make-up, as though they were going to a party, and had their hair put up in all kinds of curls and coils. At home in the village practically no one used glasses, but here many people wore glasses in all shapes and colors. At the street corner a blind man stood begging. From time to time someone put a coin in his hand. Hajdar began to feel in his belt for a coin to give him, but Saber grabbed his arm.

"He can't keep the money, anyway," he whispered in Hajdar's ear. "A rich old man has a whole bunch of beggars. He gives them a little food and makes them sleep in a small dormitory. When they get home at night he puts all their money into his own pocket."

Now they finally began to understand why foreigners called this Chicken Street. On the sidewalk lay rows of chickens and hens with their legs tied together. The customers looked them over and made their choice. Then the shop owner expertly chopped off the cackling bird's head. The street smelled rancid from the chicken flesh and feathers.

Hajdar saw several shops that did not open onto the street. Through a large glass window he could see a shopkeeper laughing at some foreign customer. Gold teeth shone in his mouth.

"Let's go in and look, Saber!"

"Are you crazy? Do you think they want ordinary Afghans in there? Father and I were almost driven out when we tried to go into one of those shops once. Anyway, we've got no time to look in shops. We'd better sell these flowers before they wilt."

The idea of standing in the middle of the crowded street and selling flowers gave Hajdar butterflies in his stomach. They had already seen some boys who were wandering up and down the street selling bunches of flowers.

Saber opened his bundle. Some of the flowers at the edge were squashed but most of them looked surprisingly fresh. Saber took fifteen small bunches in his arms and told Hajdar to stay in front of the vegetable bazaar and look after the rest.

"Sell as many as you can," was the last thing he said before he disappeared down Chicken Street.

Hajdar looked furtively at how the others went about selling their goods. Then he tied a little bundle of flowers together and thought deeply about what he should do next. It would look just great if Saber came back and he hadn't sold a single bunch. So he summoned up all his courage and shouted, "Flowers," with a voice that sounded painfully thin. Although he thought that he had really shouted, his voice was drowned out in the noise around him.

Finally a woman heard him. She had just got out of a car and was on her way into the vegetable bazaar. She turned to Hajdar and said something in a foreign language. Was she asking him how much they cost? He held up ten fingers for ten afghanis and looked a little pleading. Before he knew what was going on, she had put the money in his hand, taken the flowers and gone.

Was it so easy? Hajdar immediately began to shout with a deeper voice as he heard the others doing. Most of the time no one seemed to notice him, but from time to time he was given a quick look. The other flower sellers stared at him a little as they went past.

Hajdar's voice began to get hoarse and hollow. No customers had turned up after the first lady. He wondered how Saber was getting on. It was obvious that he hadn't sold all his bunches yet, since he hadn't come back.

"And who has said that you can stand here?" Hajdar heard a stern voice just behind him. He turned round and saw a large, heavy man who was selling vegetables.

"I'm looking after this bundle for my friend," he said quietly.

"Looking after the bundle, huh!" snorted the man. "You're standing right at the entrance to the vegetable bazaar and taking all our customers. There are enough kids around here selling flowers. If you want to sell something, you'll have to move along like everyone else." He took a threatening step toward Hajdar, who quickly gathered up the bundle and prepared to move on. But he was in such a hurry that he fumbled with the bundle, and before he knew it, the bunches of flowers were all over the street.

Hajdar felt like crying, but he knew he didn't have time for that. Quick as a flash he began to gather up the wild tulips. He had just managed to pick up half of them when he jumped at the sound of a sharp honking noise. He looked up and saw an old-fashioned bus right behind him.

The driver was shaking his fist. Suddenly Hajdar felt overwhelmingly tired and frightened. He was sorry he had ever come to Kabul. Tears welled up in his eyes.

Then he saw two hands eagerly collecting the tulips and placing them in the bundle. Surprised, Hajdar dried his eyes with his shirt sleeve. In front of him stood a pale little man. Hajdar noticed from his clothes and features that he was not an Afghan.

"Don't cry. It'll be all right," said the man without the slightest foreign accent. He handed the bundle to Hajdar, who was so surprised that he neither thanked him nor asked where he came from.

"Goodbye," shouted the man before he vanished in the mass of people.

Hajdar dried his eyes carefully. Then he clenched his teeth together and decided that now he would sell his flowers. At least he was no longer in front of the vegetable bazaar. But it seemed foolish to shout, "Flowers," when foreigners couldn't understand what he was saying. Afghans would never pay for wild flowers.

Nobody came up to him until some fat ladies streamed off the bus that had nearly run him down. They all had pale complexions, bright-red lips and yellow-white hair that looked like hay stacks on their heads. One of them came up to Hajdar, and he smiled and held up ten fingers. She slapped her hand down and held up five. He laughed and held up nine. Finally they agreed on eight afghanis. Then several of the blonde ladies came and bought bouquets for eight afghanis.

Hajdar could hardly believe his eyes. Eleven ladies from the bus each bought a bouquet.

"Russians," whispered people to each other.

So that's what they looked like — the Russians he had heard so much about. Saber used to say that he didn't know what to believe. His uncle thought that the Russians had helped Afghanistan. They had built roads, started schools and sold weapons to the Afghans. Mir thought it was lucky that Afghanistan had such a kind country on its border, but Saber's father called them heathens. That meant they did not believe in God. And that was the worst thing that could happen to anyone, he thought.

"They smell bad," he said. "Pig meat and vodka." Mir used to laugh and say that it didn't matter. The main thing was that they helped their poor neighbors.

Anyway, Hajdar thought, ordinary people didn't need to worry about such things. He stood there for a while without being approached by anyone. He began to dream of what he would do when he had bought all his buses. With his pockets full of money he would buy all the flowers from all the flower sellers on Chicken Street.

It seemed as though all Kabul's blind and lame

people had gathered together on Chicken Street. With their most pleading voices they stretched out hands and asked for money. One mother carried a dirty little child who cried constantly. She was given more money than anyone because people couldn't bear to hear the child screaming. Hajdar wondered whether the child was in pain or if the mother didn't give it food so that it would wail all the time. One just couldn't know who was really the poorest.

A man approached riding a bike. Behind him sat two small children, and a large bundle of lottery tickets hung from the handlebars. The man had no legs, but the bike pedals were attached just in front of him so that he could turn them with his hands. It looked as though he had driven around in his cart a great deal. His arms were strong and rippling with muscles.

From a cake shop a few steps away came the most wonderful smells. In the window, Hajdar could see a large swarm of flies enjoying themselves on the long rows of buns, cakes and pastries. In his village there were no ovens for baking this type of bread, and Saber had told him how wonderful the bread from Kabul tasted. Hajdar's mouth watered. It felt like a long time since he had eaten that kebab in Hadi's restaurant.

He jumped. Someone had grabbed him by the scruff of the neck.

"I see, so this is where you are," Saber laughed. He looked as though he had been running.

"You scared me! Have you sold anything?"

"Did you think I had thrown away my flowers?" Saber sneered, holding out his empty hands.

"You mean you've sold all fifteen bunches?"

"They sold like wildfire. One of the other boys taught me a few words of English, and then it was much easier."

Hajdar looked admiringly at Saber. He told him how he had sold eleven bunches to the Russians.

"You don't mean it!" Saber looked happily surprised. Then he picked up ten bouquets and disappeared again.

By now there were no more than fifteen bunches left in the bundle. Hajdar gathered the flowers together and carried them in his arms.

A truck made its way through the crowd. Water trickled down the sides. Hajdar saw that the truck was full of hard-pressed snow that must have come from the mountains. As soon as the truck stopped, shop owners streamed to it from all directions. They bought large blocks of the hard snow and put them into metal trays of soft-drink bottles.

When Saber finally returned, he had sold all his bouquets again. Hajdar had only sold three, so they decided to try to sell the rest together. Saber managed to get Hajdar to say a few sentences of English. At first his mouth felt strange pronouncing the new words. He muttered them to himself, sucking on the consonants. "Flowers, flowers. Only ten afghanis."

When they had only a few bunches left, the boys decided to stop for a rest. They walked to the bakery where people were lined up. Inside the shop Hajdar could see a man sitting in front of a large trough, forming small lumps of dough that he weighed on some scales. Another man formed the dough into flatbread, and a third man put the bread on a baker's peel, which he first wet with water. He bent over the burning hot oven in the floor, put the peel into the oven and attached the bread to the side. A fourth baker lifted out the bread with an iron hook. The breads were burning hot and golden brown. Most of the customers had bread baskets and pieces of cloth with them, but the boys had to take the bread directly in their hands. For the first few minutes they had to change hands often until the bread cooled down.

Saber led them to a park not far away, where they sat on a bench and ate the bread and a raw onion they had bought, until they felt really full. They each bought a pot of green tea from a tea house nearby.

Suddenly Saber grabbed Hajdar's arm.

"Do you know what we've forgotten?"

"No, what?"

"We should be at the bank when Mir finishes work. What if he's standing there, waiting for us?"

Now they no longer cared about the last flowers. They half ran along Chicken Street and Hajdar knocked over the tray of an old man selling dried apricots. They heard angry shouts behind them, but they didn't stop. Hajdar found it difficult to keep up with Saber, who took enormous steps.

Finally they were there. They stopped to catch their breath back. The guard who had chased Hajdar away earlier in the day was still going back and forth in front of the building, but all the doors to the bank were shut. It looked as though everyone had gone home for the day. Saber and Hajdar walked around the bank and investigated all the side roads, until the guard began to look at them suspiciously.

Finally they got up their courage and asked the guard if any of the bank's employees had waited outside after work, but the guard just shook his head.

It had begun to get dark. Saber went to the bus stop and Hajdar ran after him. Soon they were on the bus, heading toward Mir's place. They got off quite near the prison, and Saber found the way to the courtyard where Mir rented a room. They climbed the steep stairs to the outdoor wooden passageway. Saber looked relieved when he noticed a light from Mir's window. He adjusted his turban and knocked. Hajdar stood behind him in the darkness.

A strange man opened the door. Saber stood there, blinded by the strong light.

"Ohhh, s-s-sorry, is Mir at home?"

"Mir?" he said. "No one called Mir lives here." And he shut the door, leaving Hajdar and Saber standing outside in the dark.

6

In the pale light outside Mir's room, Saber was quiet. Then he turned and walked back to the stairs. Hajdar stayed close on his heels. On the way down the dark, narrow stairway they bumped into a little man in a long padded coat. He muttered something angrily, but then brightened when he recognized Saber. The man, who was the caretaker of the building, explained that Mir had moved to Kote Sangi some weeks earlier, because the landlord had wanted to raise the rent. While he talked, the old man eagerly fingered his black prayer beads. It was a little hard to understand him because he was toothless and had a mouth full of green tobacco.

"Kote Sangi," laughed Saber. "That's where we first stopped with the bus. There's a caravanserai just by the bus station. That must be where Mir lives." They followed the alley out to the main street again. On the way they came upon a bunch of wild dogs. The boys bent down to throw stones at the shabby mongrels, but the dogs were so used to having stones thrown at them that they ran before the boys could raise their arms. Saber told Hajdar about people who had been bitten by crazy dogs and had died in terrible pain. One could never be sure about wild dogs that lived on the rubbish dumps in town. They could be carrying a deadly disease.

Hajdar felt for his knife in his belt – even if he would never dare use it on a crazy dog.

They had to wait a while for the Kote Sangi bus. When they went past the prison, Hajdar caught a glimpse of a guard and his rifle, with an evil-looking bayonet attached. In the caravanserai, they asked around and soon found their way to the loft entrance to Mir's room. There was a light coming from the window.

Mir opened the door and hugged Saber. No one had told him that Saber was in town. His workmate from the bank must have forgotten the boys and the bundle under the desk.

"Come in and sit down!" Mir said to the boys. "This is my friend Anvar. He drives a taxi. You came just at the right moment. We were just going to eat something and then go to the cinema."

On a large plate in the middle of the floor lay a mountain of freshly made cheese and raisins, typical spring food. Mir wanted to hear all about Saber's family and the others in the village. Anvar described all the crazy things that happened to a taxi driver in Kabul, until Hajdar and Saber shook with laughter. Then they moved on to more serious topics. Mir told them how unfair everything was in Kabul. Anyone who didn't know powerful people was always badly treated. Things had to change soon, he said. People wouldn't put up with this forever.

Later, when they had seated themselves in the theater, Hajdar wondered whether he would be able to stay awake for the film, he was so tired. But when the strange pictures began to move on the screen, he was awake in an instant. He was in another world. He couldn't understand what the film stars said, because they spoke Hindi, but it was easy to understand the story. It was about a poor boy who swept the streets of Bombay. He wanted to marry a spoiled rich girl, but she just laughed at him. Then her father lost all his money and the poor boy turned out to be the son of a millionaire. When the girl came and pleaded on her bare knees for the boy to marry her, he married the daughter of a poor sweeper instead. The last scene showed them traveling in a large car with a chauffeur. They threw a coin in the dusty street to a girl who sat begging by the roadside. It was the same girl who had rejected the poor boy at the beginning of the film.

Hajdar would never forget the beautiful pictures of the palaces and parks in Bombay, and the Indian music and dances. At home in the village he had never suspected there was anything like this. Saber's stories were nothing compared to seeing all the glory of Kabul with his own eyes. He had heard about the town where one pressed a button and it became light, where one turned a faucet and water came. But today he had *seen* with his own eyes.

After the film they went to Hadi's kebab restaurant. Hadi waved at them but he was busy serving the other customers who streamed in from the cinema. Anvar and Mir began to joke about the picture of the president that hung so high up on the wall that it almost touched the ceiling, when Hadi's father came over and sat at their table. He was a large man in a Persian lamb cap who talked constantly and seemed to enjoy having four listeners. He told them about his life and dreamily read them poems. Hajdar decided he would get a book of poetry and begin learning poems, too, as soon as he had learned to read a bit better.

7

WHEN Hajdar woke up the next morning, the sun was high in the sky. Mir had already left for work, and Saber was trying to prepare the morning tea. About an hour later the boys were heading for Mir's bank. The bus was so packed that they stood hanging on the step outside. It was a rather dangerous way to travel, but it was free. The conductor could never manage to get to the people who were hanging outside.

"Exciting," shouted Saber into Hajdar's ear. A bit too exciting, thought Hajdar, when buses and cars coming from the other direction came dangerously near them. A brown military truck drew up beside them. On the top stood boys in gray uniforms, not much older than Saber.

Crowds of girls in black school uniforms walked along the sidewalk, shading themselves with their schoolbooks over their heads to avoid getting sunburnt. Hajdar realized that people only had to look at his dark skin to realize that he was from the country where people worked out in the sun.

Soon they arrived at the bank. The same guard was going back and forth in front of the large steps, so Hajdar stayed on the other side of the road while Saber ran into the bank. A little while later he came out with the raisins, and the boys headed for Chicken Street.

It didn't take them long to realize that they couldn't sell raisins without scales. Saber went into a shop and bought some cheap paper bags. Then he flashed his broadest smile and asked if he could borrow the shop scales for a short while. But the shopkeeper refused.

"Let's try the vegetable bazaar," suggested Hajdar, suddenly feeling more sure of himself. He went straight up to the man who had shouted at him the day before. His scales were much simpler than those in the shops; the weights were only different-sized stones. At first the man looked a little thoughtful, but he soon gave in. The boys quickly weighed the raisins into thirty bags. They gave the vegetable seller one as thanks for his help.

They soon saw that it was much easier selling flowers than raisins. Most of the foreigners weren't interested in raisins – even though they were fine light ones that had been dried in the shade instead of the sun.

All morning the boys shouted themselves hoarse. Then, disappointed, they carried their bundles back to the bank. Mir was finished early because it was Thursday – the day before Friday, which was a holiday in Afghanistan. When he heard about their bad luck, he suggested, "What do you think about going to the zoo on the way home?" And suddenly the bundles didn't seem so heavy anymore.

The weekend was over almost as soon as it had started. They saw the zoo, went to a tea house and to the cinema again. Anvar took them out in his taxi, and they had a picnic in Baburs Park, on the mountain side of the river. They ate dinner at Anvar's and met several of Mir's friends. Thursday and Friday felt like a never-ending party.

On Friday night Mir went out on an errand, and Hajdar and Saber talked about their trip home. Now they just had to get rid of all their raisins, so they could buy what they needed in town and pay for their bus tickets. Hajdar's mother had asked him to buy some tea and sugar.

As the boys were discussing their plans, the door opened, and there stood a rather breathless Mir with three flatbreads under his arm.

"Saber," he said slyly, "how would you like to stay in Kabul?"

"What do you mean?"

"What would you say if I found you a job?"

"Tell me, tell me," shouted Saber, his cheeks red with excitement.

"You'd be working at the home of a foreigner — cleaning, watering the garden, cutting the lawn and washing the car. You'll be better paid than I am at the bank."

Mir continued eagerly talking about the job he had just heard about. One of Anvar's colleagues had had the job, but now he was going to do his military service and wanted to give the job to someone he knew, so he could be sure of getting it back when he came home again.

Saber looked from Mir to Hajdar and back to Mir again. It didn't take him long to decide.

"I'll try it," he said.

All three of them were tired after a long and busy weekend, and they had hardly rolled out the mattresses and turned off the light before Mir and Saber fell asleep. But Hajdar lay tossing about, listening to the sounds from the courtyard. Some dogs were barking. Far away he could hear the noise of trucks starting up. Someone whistled. A noisy laugh echoed between the rows of houses. Two angry voices were arguing. And then it was quiet again.

Hajdar didn't know why he felt so disappointed. He knew he really should be glad for Saber. They certainly needed money for their large family. And Hajdar didn't really want to stay too long in Kabul himself. A few days or a week was all right. But in the long run, how could one live with all these people, houses and cars? Could anyone who had been born in the country ever get used to city life?

The next morning, Hajdar and Saber stood in the morning rush on the street, trying to get a place on the bus. Bus after bus went past without stopping.

Clumps of people hung outside the doors, so the buses were heavily weighted down on one side. Taxis whizzed back and forth, but the boys didn't even look to see if they were empty or not. They certainly couldn't spend their money on taxis! But to walk all the way to Chicken Street with their bundles was hard to imagine.

Just when they were wondering whether they would be waiting for a bus all day, a black-and-white taxi with squeaking brakes came to a halt just in front of them. Anvar put his happy bearded face through the window.

"Do you want a lift?" he laughed. Hajdar could see his shining gold teeth.

"Uh, we're waiting for the bus," mumbled Saber.

"Where are you going?"

"Chicken Street… but the bus is bound to come soon."

"Don't stand there talking nonsense. Just jump in. Perhaps I'll find some other passengers on the way. At least you can go free as my guests."

To ride on a bus through town was one thing. To ride in a taxi with Anvar was something else. Several times Hajdar was convinced that they would be squashed under one of the trucks or buses that they met, but Anvar always managed to swerve away at the very last second. Several times it seemed as though a pedestrian would find himself under the taxi, but in some mysterious way they got through safely.

Anvar never seemed to notice that anything dangerous was going on. With his Persian hat tilted on his head and a cigarette hanging out of the corner of his mouth, he laughed and chatted away. Soon he picked up more passengers who had been waiting by the side of the road. They bargained a little with each other before they agreed on a price and got into the car. Hajdar was glad that Anvar would at least get some money from his trip, when he had been so kind and driven them for free.

Not that the taxi was luxurious. The lock on the right front door was broken, and the door was held together with a piece of string. When there was no more room in the back, Saber and Hajdar crawled over the seat into the front. There they sat squashed together, listening to Anvar tell them about the time he had tried to brake to avoid running into a camel. When he wasn't able to swerve aside, he drove right between the camel's legs, which were left hanging over the top of the car. He drove for a while with the camel on the car, and it wasn't until he got out of the car that he saw an old man sitting on the camel. The man was quite terrified and couldn't say a word. But Anvar invited him for tea and the camel for water, and soon the pair recovered.

The boys jumped out at Chicken Street and thanked Anvar for the ride. Then they set about trying to sell their raisins.

By mid-morning they still hadn't managed to sell

a single bag. For a while they didn't bother to call out. No one seemed interested in buying anything from them, anyway.

As they stood there, an enormous car came crawling slowly along the curbside. At the wheel sat an old gray-haired lady. Hajdar couldn't get used to the idea that women drove cars — and old ladies at that. He smiled to himself at the thought of his own grandmother behind the wheel of a car. She had never even seen a car in her whole life!

The gray-haired lady had a back seat full of children of various ages. She gazed about as though she was looking for something. Then she caught sight of the boys. She smiled at them and looked interestedly at their raisins. *"Keshmesh tshand as?"* she asked.

They rushed to tell her how much the raisins cost. She made a gesture to show them that she wanted all the bags that were left and would gladly take everything in the bundle as well. At first the boys thought they had misunderstood, but once they realized that she really wanted everything, they hurried to carry the bags to her car. The children in the back immediately began to help themselves to raisins.

The gray-haired lady positively beamed at Hajdar and Saber. She paid for the raisins and didn't want any change. Then she shut the car door, started the engine and disappeared as quickly as she had come. The children in the back seat waved at the boys.

Hajdar and Saber looked at each other and

laughed. It seemed as though on Chicken Street one just didn't know what would happen next.

"I suppose we're through with our work," said Saber happily. "Let's go and rest in the park. I'm tired."

Hajdar stood quietly for a moment. "I don't want to sleep away my last afternoon in Kabul," he mumbled. "It's different for you. You don't have to leave. But who knows how long it will be before I come here again?"

So Hajdar set off on his own. He was disappointed that Saber wouldn't come with him, but at least he would show him that he could look after himself alone in town.

He went along the streets he knew so well, past Mir's bank, over a bridge and then along the river. Bright inexpensive carpets hung for sale on the stone wall along the river's edge. In one of the shops Hajdar saw expensive foreign cloth like the material Mir had in his suit. Some shop windows had different-sized knives, and Hajdar felt pleased that not one of them was as fine as his dagger. He almost forgot about Saber in the excitement of so much to see. He had never before thought that people needed so many different things, but it seemed as though there were always people with money to buy. He stayed an extra long time at the cycle bazaar. Indian businessmen with bright red turbans and rolled-up beards sat like kings among the hundreds of bikes. Nearby were the Indian spice shops with their strange exotic smells.

One bazaar led in to the next. Now Hajdar could see shop after shop with scarves, bracelets, turbans and rolls of cloth, so he bought some cheap bracelets for Fatima and local sweets for his mother and grandmother.

Suddenly he found himself in the strangest bazaar he had come to so far. It sounded as though he had entered a grove of trees on a spring day. Birdsong came toward him from every direction. There were birds of every size and color – green parrots, brown speckled hunting falcons, chickens and dwarfturkeys, yellow canaries that cost a small fortune and sang divinely.

Hajdar had to stop and hold his breath. It must sound just like this in Paradise, he thought. Not all the birds sang and not all of them sang beautifully, but together they sounded like a perfect orchestra.

He soon noticed that one bird sang more beautifully than any other. He tried to follow its song, but became confused by the sound of the other birds. Then he caught sight of it – a little gray bird that trilled more clearly and beautifully than a canary.

All of a sudden Hajdar felt an overwhelming desire to hold the bird for just a minute. He stretched out his hand toward the birdcage and carefully opened the little door.

"Leave my cages alone, kid." He heard a voice

right behind him that made him jump. At the same moment the bird became frightened and quickly flew out through the open door.

The man who shouted tried to catch it, but the bird disappeared under the bazaar's cloth roof. Hajdar forgot everything else and ran, his eyes following the flight of the bird. Why had he been so foolish?

He heard the man's footsteps behind him but rushed on after the flapping bird. Several times he almost stumbled. He kept his eyes fixed on the gray bird, which seemed to be moving farther away from him. He had to catch it.

All at once Hajdar felt a burning pain in his right eye. He stopped. The bird disappeared. His eye felt as though knives were going into it. He pressed the palm of his hand against his eye and felt something wet running down his cheek. Blood!

Then everything went black.

8

As though in a dream, Hajdar heard voices.
"He let one of my songbirds out."

"But look how his eye's bleeding."

"Yes, that's a punishment for not being able to keep his fingers to himself."

"But he's fainted," a woman's voice said.

"Of course. He was chasing that bird and ran right into the pole that was sticking out from the shop."

"Poor child! What if it has blinded him?"

With a little effort Hajdar opened his eyes and began to stand up. A sigh came from the crowd.

"The bird," he said. "Where did the bird go?"

Someone gave Hajdar a piece of cloth to wipe the blood off his face. He held it against his eye, which still burned terribly. His thoughts flew to the one-eyed man grilling kebab at Hadi's restaurant. Would he look like that for the rest of his life? If only Saber were here!

"He must go to a doctor," someone shouted, and other voices agreed.

"Take him to the eye hospital," suggested a man with a deep voice.

It wasn't long before a taxi came crawling into the narrow alley. Someone handed the driver the money for the trip. The driver assured Hajdar that everything would turn out all right, and that he was lucky to have had the accident in Kabul, which had the only eye hospital in the country. There were clever doctors there who could certainly fix his eye again.

Hajdar was glad when the taxi started to move more quickly. Now the pain wasn't quite so bad when he pressed the cloth against his eye, but his head felt as though it would split into a thousand pieces. He hoped they would get there soon.

They drew up in front of a large gate. Inside Hajdar could see a large gray building.

"Well, I can't drive you any farther," the driver said. "They've already paid your fare, so just go through the gate and main entrance to the hospital. It'll be all right, I'm sure." He gave Hajdar an encouraging thump on the back, which the boy felt right through his head.

It'll be all right, it'll be all right. The words echoed and thudded in Hajdar's head. When he held the cloth against his injured eye, he could see sparkling suns and stars in all the colors of the rainbow. His knees felt weak, but he kept on walking toward the main entrance.

He came into a large waiting room where people sat on benches, on the floor or stood packed tightly waiting for their turn. He felt that everyone was staring at him. His head was spinning. He grabbed hold of a bench just as he was about to fall.

"Poor child," he heard a friendly female voice say. She reminded him of his mother. "Have you come here all by yourself? Come with me and we'll find a nurse."

Later Hajdar could only remember vaguely what happened next. People in white coats looked after him. A doctor examined his injured eye and looked very serious.

"We must operate at once," he said. But it seemed to Hajdar that it took ages before he lay on the operating table. The operation took a long time, but at least it didn't hurt. *It'll be all right, it'll be all right,* pounded in his head.

Through his healthy eye he could vaguely see the green operating clothes as though through a fog. Afterward when he thought about the eye operation, it was just eyes he remembered, peering at him above the surgical masks. Tired eyes, happy eyes, angry eyes, sad eyes.

He was given a sparkling white bandage for his eye and was told that he must not remove it for ten days. Then he was to return to the hospital, and they would see if the operation had been a success.

If it had been a success.

Hajdar rested on a bed in a room on his own for a few hours. He must have slept, because he woke with a start when someone gently shook him by the shoulder. His eye didn't hurt very much, but he was given a prescription to take to the hospital pharmacy, where he could get some pills to take when his eye started to hurt a bit later.

Dusk had fallen by the time Hajdar left the hospital. The guard at the door helped him hail a taxi, and the boy had almost fallen asleep on the soft back seat by the time they got to Mir's yard.

He walked with heavy steps to the passageway and desperately hoped that someone was home. Light shone from the window. He knocked.

Saber opened the door. "Saber," said Hajdar, "I don't think I'll go home tomorrow." Then he sank down onto one of the mattresses on the floor to answer the questions that fell all around him.

The days went slowly for Hajdar. Mir went to work at the bank as usual, and Saber began a new life working for the foreigners. Mir's friend was beginning his national service in a week, so until then he and Saber were working together.

Hajdar was homesick as he had never been before. He slept as much as possible and tried to read some of Mir's magazines and books, but they were too hard, and his healthy eye got tired too quickly. Several times a day he would take short walks, but he never took the bus to the town center alone. After his accident, he no longer yearned to go to the bazaars. When he did go out, people came up to him and touched his bandage, so that it became more gray than white. He felt like one of the animals in the zoo. From time to time he went to see Hadi just around the corner. Sometimes Hadi could sit down and chat, but generally he only had time to say hello before he had to rush off to the next table.

If the days were long and boring, the evenings with Saber and Mir were much more fun. Mir would bring home sweet things to go with the tea and teach the boys how to play backgammon and chess. One evening Mir's friends came by with different instruments. They played so loudly that the whole passageway vibrated.

Saber would come home and tell the strangest stories about the house he worked in. Hajdar didn't know how much of it he should believe, but Saber assured him that every word was true. Those foreigners really behaved strangely. Most of their food was not bought at the bazaar but at another shop where only foreigners were allowed. The meat they ate came in small metal tins which they opened with a type of knife. There were many water faucets in the house, and even warm water came out of some of them. But they always boiled the water before they drank it. They drank coffee practically all the time instead of tea. They had a cook to make their meals, and he told Saber even more incredible stories. Even though the foreigners were rich, they owned few proper carpets. Instead there were lots of chairs and tables everywhere, but not a single mattress on the floor to sit on comfortably. They sat and dangled their legs from the chairs.

One day Saber came home beaming. He told Hajdar that the people he worked for were going to India for a week, so the next day Hajdar could be with him at work for the whole day.

Hajdar had never seen such large glass windows. Like shop windows, they stretched over one whole side of the house. Inside the walls was a green and luxuriant garden with vines and fruit trees. Hajdar jumped when a large dog suddenly came bounding up to them in the garden. He immediately thought about everything he had heard about wild dogs. Desperately he ran toward the gate in the garden wall. The dog followed close behind, and Hajdar pulled in vain at the locked gate. He turned around to see Saber standing there with a broad grin on his face.

"You don't need to be scared of that dog! They keep it inside. It even sleeps in their bedroom. He's called Lassie."

Hajdar couldn't believe his ears. Who would have thought that there were people with such peculiar ideas? Dogs inside. Grandmother and Mother had always told him that dogs were unclean animals. And did people actually give names to dogs? After this he would never be surprised by anything again.

Saber took him on a tour of the house, and it was just as strange as Saber had described it. Pictures hung on the walls, but you couldn't tell what they represented. And the toilet was in the house instead of out in the yard.

Saber said that the foreigners didn't take their shoes off before going indoors, and that they would sit and show the dirty soles of their shoes to each other instead of sitting with crossed legs like decent people.

Hajdar was only allowed to watch when Saber washed the foreigners' big car. Saber said that it was too easy to scratch the color. It made no difference how much Hajdar promised to be careful. The man who had worked before Saber had scratched the car so badly once that he had nearly lost his job.

After Saber had finished cleaning the car, Hajdar followed him into the garage where there was a little room with an electric burner on the floor. The spiral ring began to glow as soon as Saber put the plug in. He boiled a large pan of water and made tea, and then they drank it in the spring sunshine outside the garage.

After they had their tea, the boys helped each other pull a machine that cut the grass. Hajdar said that he could do it just as well with a little sickle, the way he did at home, but Saber explained that the foreigners liked the lawn even and fine. They raked up the grass and took it out to the sidewalk outside the garden wall. Before the end of day some shepherd boy would come by with his flock of sheep, and there wouldn't be a blade left.

Hajdar helped Saber weed the garden. He was used to this type of work, and he enjoyed the smell of the wet earth. It reminded him of the village. Town was so full of strange smells, especially the smell of car exhaust fumes. But the strangest thing about town was that the air was filled with so many smells at the same time.

"Can you imagine staying in town forever like Mir?" Hajdar asked Saber.

"I don't know yet," answered Saber thoughtfully. "I suppose one can get to like it."

Did that mean that Saber and he would go separate ways? Could he imagine staying in town some time in the future? It was good to be only ten years old and not have to decide for a while. Hajdar knew his mother would certainly not let him live in town for a few years yet.

9

THE next morning it took Hajdar nearly an hour to go from Mir's house to the eye hospital. It was finally time to have his bandage taken off. He could hear his heart thumping in his chest as he walked through the large doors to the waiting room.

This time Hajdar had to wait like all the other patients. After a while a bench came free and he sat with his legs drawn up under him. Soon a boy of about his own age sat next to him. He told Hajdar that he had traveled from the mountains for several days to get to the hospital. The boy said there used to be a little hospital up in the mountains, but people in Kabul were jealous that the best doctors worked there, so they closed the hospital down. Now all the sick people had to make their way to the capital. Most of them didn't have the strength to make such a long trip, but he just had a pain in his eyes. He was afraid he would go blind if he didn't see a doctor. At home in his village the Muslim priest had tried all the tricks and magic he knew, but nothing worked.

"You'll see, it'll be all right," said Hajdar encouragingly. Then he almost bit his tongue. Maybe this boy would go blind. Maybe Hajdar himself would be blind in his right eye when they removed the bandage. Why should his eye be fine when so many people went blind?

Finally it was Hajdar's turn. He held his breath when they began to ease off the bandage. They had told him to cover his left eye at the same time. It was quite dark, and he wondered for a while if this was how it felt to be blind.

The doctor carefully lifted away the last layer of bandage. His eye hurt because it was so unused to the light. He blinked several times and his eyelid felt a bit stiff. But... he could see — at first a little hazily but then clearer and clearer.

The doctor and nurse looked pleased. They told him he must not get dust or dirt in his eye and that he should come back for a check-up in a few weeks. It had all gone unusually well so far.

Hajdar danced happily out along the hospital corridors and through the waiting room. What did he care if everyone stared? He squinted when he came out into the daylight and was grateful that the clouds were covering the sun for the time being. At a half-trot he went to the house where Saber worked and told him the good news. They hugged each other and laughed so loudly that the cook peered out from behind the drapes. When he found out what was going on, he took steaming hot cinnamon buns from the oven and placed a big pile of them on a plate. A short while later Hajdar and Saber sat by the garage wall with a pot of tea each and their mouths full of cinnamon buns.

They had never tasted anything like it.

Days grew into weeks. Hajdar's injured eye felt better and better. He looked happily at his face in Mir's mirror. The swelling in the eye had subsided, and the red scar on the eyelid was the only thing that bore witness to the accident in the bird market.

Now Hajdar was with Saber during the days. The foreigners had come back, but they didn't object to the boys sharing the work. Hajdar was even given a tip from time to time. It felt good to be able to buy some small things to take home to Mir, since they had been living with him for so long now.

The last time Hajdar was at the hospital, the doctor looked at him seriously.

"Do you know it is a miracle that you can see with your right eye?" he said.

Hajdar fingered the edge of his turban awkwardly.

"We never thought we could save the eye, and even wondered about surgically removing it. Just make sure this never happens again. I can't promise you the same luck next time."

Hajdar went backward and bowed as he left the room. Then he disappeared out the door, along the corridors and out into the fresh air. He breathed deeply a few times. It felt good to be alive.

10

THE next day was Thursday. Mir finished early at the bank, so the boys decided to join him to visit a little fair that was held just behind the old bazaars. As the three of them walked through the bazaars toward the fair, they were so busy talking that they nearly fell over boiled, grinning sheeps' heads that lay in rows on a piece of cloth on the sidewalk. Red wild tulips had been placed between the teeth of the skinned and cooked heads, and a man stood nearby, ladling squash from a large glass jar. It was made of raisins and water that had been boiled together. Saber proudly took out his newly earned money and bought three glasses.

Suddenly, from a long way off came what sounded like thunder. Hajdar looked up at the sky, but it was clear blue, so they continued on their way.

"The fair is just at the end of this street," Saber explained excitedly.

Boom! They looked up at the sky and then at each other. Mir stood still, looking confused. A large black cloud rose above the houses.

"I wonder where the fire is," he said pensively. Just then, several military trucks drove through the little alley, not even slowing down in spite of all the people. Serious-looking soldiers in worn gray uniforms stood herded together on the back of the trucks.

Hajdar heard several loud explosions, and he could see smoke. Suddenly people moved much more quickly along the alleyways. Some half ran and looked worriedly behind them.

"Don't you think we should go home?" Hajdar asked carefully.

"What, and not go to the fair when we're so close?" Saber said in a disappointed tone.

"We'll carry on as long as it doesn't get worse than this," Mir said calmly. "We can always go into one of the shops." But he had hardly finished speaking when shop owners began to gather their goods together and shut their stores with large padlocks.

Now the sky was dark with smoke. Mir suddenly looked serious.

"We'll have to go to the fair another day. Perhaps we should do what Hajdar suggests and make our way home." They followed the stream of people from the little alley into the large street. A blind beggar tried to ask people what was going on, but no one had time to stop. They hurried on.

In the crush someone had knocked over the squash man's table, but he didn't have time to pick up the broken jars. He just attached his table to his back and began to run along the street.

Cars hooted as they drove bumper to bumper. A tank made its way between the lines of traffic, and several trucks full of military personnel suddenly appeared. Mir seemed quite calm, but he took hold of Saber's and Hajdar's hands. Hajdar noticed that Mir's hand was sweaty.

"Come, we'll take a back alley instead," Mir suggested. They went into the alley again and found an almost deserted back street that ran parallel to the main road. Mir had to let go of their hands because the street was so narrow. Behind them they could still hear explosions from time to time. Then they heard a new noise. Mir said it was the sound of machine guns. They were half running onward, and Hajdar found it a little difficult to keep up with the others. They turned into an alley on the right and were soon back on the main street. Now Mir held firmly onto both boys.

"Over there is the bus stop," he said and squeezed their hands. But while they stood there, several buses went past. Some were weighted down very heavily with all the passengers who hung outside the doors. Others were quite empty and went past quickly without opening their doors. It was the same with the taxis. They were either packed tight or drove past empty and locked.

"We can't stay here," Mir said. "The buses will never come. I don't think it's a good idea to go over the big bridge where the cars are driving right now,

85

but we must get over the river. There's a little wooden bridge down this way."

They finally reached the wooden bridge after many twisting paths, and were soon on the street that led to the caravanserai where Mir lived. At one place a tank was parked in the middle of the road. Hundreds of curious people stood crowded together on the sidewalk, watching it. Every now and then the turret of the tank would twirl around, and the barrel would sweep over the spectators' heads.

Mir was walking faster and faster, and was now practically dragging the boys after him. He tried to find a back alley again where it was a little calmer, but guards were posted on every little street to force people to remain on the main road.

Finally they approached Mir's yard. Almost all the shops were locked. The cinema was shut. It was absolutely quiet in Hadi's restaurant. The picture of the president shone in the sunlight that poured in through the restaurant windows.

They entered the yard and ran up the stairs to the hall. Several of the doors to various rooms were open, and people stood talking in subdued voices. Hajdar and Saber went into Mir's room and lay down on the floor pillows, while Mir went out and talked to some of his neighbors. Even at this distance they could hear the noise of the explosions and machine-gun fire.

"Are you frightened?" Hajdar asked Saber after a while.

"A bit. And I think Mir is, too."

Mir came in and shut the door. He told them what the neighbors had told him. Some said that it was just a military exercise. Others said that the president was getting rid of some enemies. Someone had actually whispered that maybe the president was dead. But they all agreed that it was safest to stay indoors.

Mir began to cook some food, but Saber and Hajdar weren't hungry. The noise kept getting closer, until the whole house was shaking. Everyone wondered if their house would be the next to be hit.

It sounded as though the explosions and the gunfire were coming from all different directions, and now they could hear airplanes, too. Hajdar was used to hearing airplane noise as a faraway throbbing, but now it came so close that he had to cover his ears.

There was a knock at the door. Before Mir had time to open it, Anvar came in. He looked as though nothing had happened.

"How are you all? The noise is really terrible. I had to stop work earlier than usual because the roads were closed. Do you know what those planes are doing? They're going round and round bombing the president's palace. You mark my words. No one knows how this is going to end. There are tanks shooting all around the palace." Anvar took off his Persian cap and scratched his head. "I have never in my life driven so much. People have been just dying to get home, and there haven't been enough taxis. But I've made a fortune!" He happily waved a bundle of notes.

They had some tea. Hajdar wondered if he was the only one listening to the noise outside. He jumped every time the window panes shook but hoped that no one noticed. For the first time he couldn't laugh at Anvar's stories.

Now it was pitch-black outside, but the battle was raging as never before. Anvar suggested they go out onto the roof to watch. Hajdar didn't want to seem like a coward, so he went with them. From the rooftop they could see missiles shooting up like fiery arrows over the city when the planes dived. They saw small flames converge over the roofs in some places. Otherwise it was dark in most of the town.

Back in the room, Mir managed to light a gas lamp. The electricity was gone. They sat and talked long into the night and pretended not to hear the noises outside. No one wanted to go to bed. In the small hours of the morning Anvar decided to stay at Mir's for the rest of the night, so all four of them stretched out on the mattresses and tried to sleep. Every time Hajdar was about to fall asleep, he woke up with a jolt. Somewhere another bomb was exploding. Between the bangs he could hear the reconnaissance planes circling the town. He wondered whether they were carrying bombs, too. What if they pressed the button just as they flew over Mir's yard? Hajdar wondered how it must feel to die. What would they say at home in the village if he and Saber were killed? How would Mother, Fatima and Grandmother manage?

The next morning, while Mir and Anvar slept, Hajdar and Saber went up onto the roof, expecting to see the town in ruins. But Kabul looked just like it had the morning before. Smoke was rising from the bakers' chimneys. People were moving about on the street. The only thing that was different was the presence of tanks in the street, and low-flying jets that occasionally circled the town, splitting the air with an ear-deafening sound.

And in the large parking lot, the buses stood still — an unusual sight.

As they stood there, looking down at the enormous parking lot, they suddenly caught sight of the bus driver who had driven them to Kabul.

"Abdul Ali, Abdul Ali!" shouted Saber as loudly as he could. "We're here, up on the roof."

Abdul Ali caught sight of them and beckoned to them with his large hand. In the parking lot, he hugged them so hard that they could hear their ribs being squeezed.

"Are you still in town? Did you ever sell your flowers and raisins?" Abdul Ali wondered if the boys were going home soon. If so, he said he would be glad to take them. He thought it safest not to travel today, but perhaps he would leave some time the next morning if everything was all right.

Mir and Anvar looked up, quite wide awake, when Hajdar and Saber came back to the room. As the boys were telling them about meeting Abdul Ali, they heard some anxious knocking at the door. One of the neighbors popped his head in to tell them what he had just heard on the radio — the president had been shot, and the people's government had taken power.

Mir and Anvar just nodded, but when the door shut, they flew into each other's arms and screamed and laughed like crazy. They rolled about on the floor. Hajdar and Saber stared at each other in shock, until Mir and Anvar noticed their expressions.

"You kids don't understand," said Mir, sitting up. "We have waited years for this to happen. Afghanistan is free at last. Just wait and see how great it will be for all of us!" Then Anvar and Mir talked for a long time about how unfair everything had been. Now everyone would have the chance to learn to read, all the farmers would have their own plots of land, and the rich people would have to share their wealth.

"This we must celebrate, gentlemen," announced Anvar. "Allow me to invite you all to partake of two giant kebabs each."

A little while later they were seated once more at Hadi's kebab restaurant. Through the window

Hajdar saw people walking about as usual. The large tanks and still buses seemed to be the only reminders of what had happened.

Then he glanced up at the wall toward the ceiling.

Where the picture of the president had hung yesterday was now an empty nail and a large light patch.

11

EARLY the next morning, Hajdar ran down to the parking lot to look for Abdul Ali's bus. He knocked on the driver's window, and Abdul Ali's tired face looked up grumpily, but his expression softened when he saw Hajdar. He said it would be several hours before he set off, and he promised not to leave without Hajdar.

Mir said goodbye before he left for the bank. Saber said that he would go to his work and ask for the morning off. After all, someone had to see Hajdar off!

The morning hours passed. Hajdar didn't have much to pack. He went down to say goodbye to Hadi, and they promised to meet when Hajdar next came to Kabul. In his mind, he wondered how long that would be. Would his mother ever let him go away again after everything that had happened?

Passengers began to climb on Abdul Ali's bus. Many people were eager to get away from town before the troubles began again. It wouldn't take long now for the bus to fill up. Then Abdul Ali would have to leave, so he wouldn't have to drive for too long in the dark before getting to Kandahar. The sun was high in the sky, but Saber still hadn't turned up. Hajdar didn't understand why it was taking such a long time to get here from the foreigners' house. Perhaps they hadn't allowed him the time off. Why should they care that he and Saber might not meet again for several years?

"I'm afraid I can't wait any longer," said Abdul Ali. "We've a long way to drive before it gets dark."

Hajdar felt a big lump in his throat as he turned to Abdul Ali. "We'd better get going, then. He's not coming."

Abdul Ali got out the crank and the engine started with a roar. All the passengers read their Arabic prayers for a safe journey. Hajdar kept looking out the window. The bus had just begun to move when...

"Stop, Abdul Ali! He's coming!" shouted Hajdar. And Saber came running toward them. When he got to the bus, he was too breathless to talk. He just lifted something up through the bus window to Hajdar, who was too surprised to say anything.

"From Mir and me," panted Saber, just as the bus began to move off again.

In Hajdar's hands was a bird cage, and in the cage was a little gray bird that sang the most beautiful song.

When he first caught sight of the mass of small low huts of his village, Hajdar saw them with eyes of a stranger. What a lot of air and freedom there was here. It was all so quiet, but how tiny the huts seemed out on the wide plain.

As soon as Hajdar came into the village, the small children crowded around him. He walked as fast as he could, but even so he seemed to collect more and more children. Mother, Fatima and Grandmother made him feel really welcome. Nothing special had happened at home in the village, but they had a thousand questions to ask about Kabul. Why hadn't Saber come home with him? Why had he stayed so long? Was it true that there was a new king in Kabul? The songbird made a big impression on them. It had been quiet during the trip, but began to sing as soon as Hajdar brought it into the house. So then he had to tell them about the bird bazaar and the eye hospital. Just as he had thought, his mother said that was the end of trips to Kabul for him. She also told him that Saber's parents had become so worried by the news on the radio that Saber's father had gone to Kabul earlier that day.

Finally Fatima couldn't contain herself any longer.

"What have you brought for us?" she asked.

"I brought myself," he teased. But her eyes shone when she saw the bracelets, and Grandmother and Mother seemed to like their sweets, which they served with tea a bit later.

That evening, Hajdar ran over to visit Saber's family, and then went on to see friends. He proudly showed off his bird, and told everyone the story of his accident and the eye operation and the troubles in Kabul.

It felt good to be the center of attention. Hajdar noticed how his story became a little more exciting every time he repeated it. Before this his dagger had been the only thing he had to boast about, but now even the older boys looked at him with admiration.

In the weeks that followed, one day was much like the next. Hajdar helped his uncles with the land as much as he could. The harvest seemed to be good, and he became more and more convinced that he belonged here and nowhere else. He hoped Saber would realize that, too.

Saber's father came home after a few days and reported that Mir and Saber were well. It was relatively quiet in Kabul, even if one saw tanks on the streets and it was still forbidden to go out at night. Saber enjoyed his job and thought he would stay. Saber's father said that the man who had had Saber's job had disappeared. He had been a part of a group of soldiers who guarded the presidential palace. On the radio they said that practically no one had been killed, but others said that trucks loaded with dead soldiers had driven away from the palace the morning after the president had been shot. Hajdar couldn't imagine that anyone had come out alive from the palace. He had seen with his own eyes how the planes attacked with missiles time after time.

If that man had disappeared, then Saber could probably stay in Kabul as long as he wanted, Hajdar thought with disappointment.

Every evening Hajdar went over to Saber's house and listened to the radio news from Kabul. There were many words he didn't understand, but he was happy to hear how good everything was going to be in Afghanistan. They often said how unfair the president and the king before him had been. Now everyone would have the chance to learn to read, and Afghanistan would decide on its own future without other countries getting involved.

The hot summer came with its sandstorms every afternoon. Even if one stayed indoors and shut all the doors and shutters, dust worked its way into every corner. So Hajdar and the others began working early in the morning before it became too hot. Once the dust storms were over, the evenings were pleasant. The flies calmed down at night, so they could sit on the roof and drink tea. On the hottest nights, the whole family would sleep on the roof.

Then it was harvest time — the busiest time of the year. Bent forward with a scythe, cutting down the hard stalks of wheat. Going round and round for days with the oxen and threshing the wheat. Then the earth had to be plowed and prepared for the following year's seed.

When night fell, Hajdar collapsed on his mattress and sometimes didn't even have the strength to eat.

He thought a little jealously of Saber's work in Kabul. *He* never needed to feel his body ache after a strenuous day. And of course he was given money at the end of each month.

When people sat and ate their bread in town, they never thought about all the work that lay behind one loaf. To sow, water, harvest, grind and bake. Perhaps that was why bread always tasted better in the village.

The days grew shorter and the nights colder. Then, suddenly, one day there stood Saber. He had been given a few days off and had come home to the village to see everyone. Many people wanted to visit with him, but he and Hajdar still spent a lot of time together.

Saber told Hajdar that he didn't see so much of Mir anymore. Mir was often at party meetings and had become one of the most important bosses at the big bank where he worked. Anvar was busy, too, going on courses and learning how Afghanistan would become a free country. He had begun to learn Russian, because he said that all schoolchildren would be forced to read it in a few years.

Mir's friend who had been imprisoned had been released, and Mir had fixed him up with a good job at the bank. Saber spent most of his free time at the kebab restaurant. He knew Hadi and his father so well that he could sit there without ordering anything.

Saber also told Hajdar about going with Mir to

see the presidential palace. People crowded round to see all the things the president and his family had acquired with the money from the poor. At the entrance was a carpet with the president's picture on it. It had probably hung on a wall in a stateroom before, but now people used it to wipe their feet on. The new president had lived in an ordinary clay house, although now he had moved into the palace himself, so one couldn't go in and look around there anymore.

Saber returned to Kabul, and Hajdar waited for the long cold winter. Every day his mother lit a coal fire under a little table in the middle of the floor. She would place a large blanket over the table, and they would sit warming their feet under the blanket. Sometimes at night they slept like that, too.

Spring and summer came around again. Saber's father went to Kabul a few times, but he never had much to tell them when he got back.

"Mir and Saber are well," was the only thing he would say. But Saber's mother told Bibigoll that Mir and Saber's father didn't agree anymore. Saber's father had even thought about bringing Saber back to the village, and Saber's mother was frightened that their boy would turn out like Mir.

On the radio they talked a lot about how the rich landowners would lose their power and the peasants would take over the land. In Hajdar's village they hadn't noticed anything like that yet, but the man who worked for the landowner was a little more careful when he demanded the khan's part of the harvest. He had a lot of bad things to say about the government, especially the new president. The Muslim priest muttered that Afghanistan was on the way to being a heathen land, whatever that meant.

Every night Hajdar listened to the radio at Saber's house. The news said things were getting better day by day, but because Afghanistan had many enemies — both abroad and at home — everyone had to help and get rid of the enemies so freedom would win.

From other villages came rumors that masses of people in the border areas had fled. Other rumors said that many villages that had helped resist the government had been bombed.

Saber came home for a few days in the fall. He had changed a lot in the past year. He had grown and his voice had become much deeper, but he also looked very serious. He said that there were often troubles in Kabul, and one still wasn't allowed to be out after eleven o'clock at night. Many people had disappeared without a trace. Some of them had been in the resistance movement against the government, but many were people who couldn't even read and understood nothing of politics. Sometimes schoolchildren and adults were forced out on the streets to demonstrate for the government, whether they wanted to or not.

"Hajdar, I just don't know what to believe," Saber

whispered. "Mir says everything will be all right once all the opponents of the system have been crushed. But Father says the president is a heathen who doesn't believe in God and who's working for the Russians."

Hajdar had never seen Saber like this before. His friend always had the answer to everything. When it was time for Saber to return to Kabul, Hajdar went with him to the main road. As the bus drew away on the other side of the mountain, Hajdar vowed that this time they wouldn't wait a whole year before meeting again.

12

THAT fall things suddenly started happening in the village. It was rumored that Saber's father was helping the guerrillas — people who wanted to get rid of the president and his government. They hid in the mountains and attacked the government soldiers whenever they had a chance. In villages where there were people who didn't like the government, the resistance men were given food before they disappeared into the mountains where no one could find them.

There were also rumors that some of the farmers helped the guerrillas in their nightly fights.

Hajdar found it more and more difficult to understand what was going on. On the radio they said that rich landowners were helping Afghanistan's enemies. But Saber's father certainly wasn't rich.

Hajdar tried to talk with Saber's father about this a few times, but he noticed that Saber's father wasn't entirely sure whether he could trust him. He couldn't talk to Mother and Fatima, since they understood nothing of life outside the village. Hajdar realized he was only eleven years old and hadn't gone to school much, but nevertheless it seemed to him that not many men in the village knew as much as he did about what went on in the world.

During the fall there was much more talk about weapons and battles. It was hard to know what was true. Some said that a village not far from theirs had been attacked by government troops. On the radio they said that the president had been sick and died, and some other person had become president instead.

Hajdar wished he could talk to Saber about everything he didn't understand.

One night as Hajdar lay in bed, half sleeping, he heard the noise of a plane far away. Drowsily he noticed that the noise was getting louder, until all at once he was wide awake and sitting straight up on his mattress.

Something wasn't right. Suddenly it felt as though the whole world was going to pieces. It felt like knives in his ears. The floor shook under him, and a blinding light came through the little window. There was an ear-deafening noise and then the sound of a plane, which quickly disappeared. It was absolutely quiet for a few moments. Then he heard Fatima's worried voice in the dark.

"Hajdar, what's happened?"

Mother tried to stop him from leaving the house, but he pulled away and disappeared outside. In the light from the stars he saw that a large part of the wall had collapsed.

He ran on with a pounding heart. There was a fire somewhere, and he ran toward the flames.

It was Saber's house.

When Hajdar returned home much later, he saw from the light of the gas lamp that Mother, Fatima and Grandmother were sitting huddled together in a corner of the room. They didn't say anything but looked at him with large questioning eyes.

"Saber's mother and some of his brothers and sisters will be sleeping here tonight. Their house has been bombed and is still burning. Saber's father and several brothers and sisters are... they are dead."

That night and the following day were like a bad dream. The morning light showed that only a few huts in the village had escaped destruction. Many people had been killed. That morning they were all buried in the little graveyard on the edge of the village. It felt like a nightmare to hear the crying and wailing rising toward the heavens all at the same time

Saber's mother cried, too, but she hadn't really had time to understand what had happened. She had already fixed some thick material in a corner of the mud hut that had escaped the bomb, so they at least had somewhere to sleep at night. All around the village, people worked to create some shelter. They dug out flour from the ruins and soon smoke came from the bread ovens. Life had to go on, even though it would never be the same again.

Saber's mother kept talking about Saber in Kabul.

She wondered who would tell him the terrible news. Deep inside Hajdar knew that Saber should be told by someone who could comfort him at the same time, but how could he leave his family in these worrying times?

Stubbornly he picked out some of the fallen stones from the clay wall. Dust rose like a cloud around him. He worked himself into a sweat carrying away bits of the wall in buckets made from car tires.

"Hajdar!" He heard his mother calling from the house and turned around. She continued in a softer voice. "Saber's mother wants to talk to you!"

"Do I have to go to Kabul?"

His mother nodded.

The next day, the trip to Kabul passed all too quickly, and soon Hajdar found himself getting off the bus in the large parking lot. As he walked toward Hadi's restaurant across the street, it seemed as if time had stood still here. As usual Hadi ran between the tables like a shuttle, and the one-eyed man steadily fanned the kebab skewers.

"Isn't Saber with you?" Hadi asked as soon as they had greeted one another.

"What are you talking about?"

"He went home to the village a couple of weeks ago."

"Home to the village? Isn't he still living here?"

Hadi stared at Hajdar for a long moment. Then

he put down everything he'd been carrying and sat down at the table. Quietly he told Hajdar that Mir had been in prison for several months. Saber hadn't wanted to tell his family the news.

"Why did they put him in prison?" asked Hajdar.

"Sssh!" Hadi lifted a finger in warning and looked worriedly around him. He lowered his voice even more. "They say it was Anvar who went to the secret police and informed on him. They had been arguing, and Anvar was nervous that Mir would get him in trouble, so that's why he went to the police himself."

"But what did Mir do?"

"Don't you understand? People don't go to prison because they have done something. They just go to prison. Father has been interrogated several times. He meets too many people from different parts of the country and gets to know what's going on everywhere."

"But what's happened to Mir? Is he still in prison?"

"At the beginning Saber went there with clean clothes several times a week. He was never allowed to see Mir, but he always got the dirty clothes back and washed them. After a month or so, no dirty clothes came anymore. Then they displayed a long list in the town. It was like a big poster with the names of all those they had killed in prison. At first Saber didn't want to go and look, but one day he plucked up his courage, and there was Mir's name."

Hajdar said nothing while Hadi told him how Saber had thought about going back to the village and telling everyone what had happened. But he had gone on working for the foreigners for a few weeks instead, until they were suddenly ordered to get out of Afghanistan within a week. They had packed and gone, leaving Saber without any work. In a few days he had sold Mir's things and everything he had been given by the foreigners. He had said that he was going home to the village. Surely nothing had happened to him on the way?

Hajdar decided that the best thing to do was to go home right away. Back at the bus station, he was wandering around the parking lot looking for a bus, when he heard a happy voice behind him.

"Well, hello, there. Look who's here!" It was Anvar, as large as life as ever.

"Hello," Hajdar answered carefully.

"Do you want a ride?"

Hajdar stood there as stiff as a rod and looked at the ground. He felt ill when he thought about what Anvar had done. At the same time, fear crept along his backbone. If Anvar had sent Mir to prison, he could no doubt do the same thing to Hajdar.

"Aren't you going to answer?" laughed Anvar.

"Of course," Hajdar said, squeezing out a smile.

"Jump in, then!"

Anvar joked and chattered, but he didn't mention Mir or Saber. As they drove around, the town looked much the same, except for the red flags and red banners with enormous letters on the walls.

The taxi had to slow down when they got caught up in a demonstration. A squeaky girl's voice was shouting, and hundreds of schoolgirls were answering in chorus.

"Long live our great leader! Death to the enemies of the people!"

Anvar wound down his window to hear better, and suddenly Hajdar noticed what a beautiful car he was sitting in. It was quite different from Anvar's old taxi with the broken front door.

"Nice car you've got yourself, Anvar."

"Times change, my boy!" Anvar flashed him a satisfied smile and asked Hajdar where he wanted to be driven.

"Here," said Hajdar without thinking. He muttered thank you, shut the car door behind him and made his way through the crowd of shouting schoolgirls in their black uniforms. If he had stayed in that car one more minute, he would have been sick.

Mir's murderer, he thought, as he began to run back to the bus station.

13

FATIMA, Bibigoll and Hajdar got up and continued after their rest on the cliff ledge. Hajdar's body ached all over, but he knew that for Mother and Fatima's sake he had to keep going, the way Father would have done.

"Hajdar," whispered Fatima eagerly. "We're not going up anymore."

He had been so deep in his own thoughts that he hadn't noticed. As usual, Fatima was right. It really looked as though they had reached the pinnacle of the mountain pass.

He began to trot down the path from pure happiness, until Fatima reminded him that Mother couldn't move as fast as they could. It was difficult to go so slowly when the path was finally going downhill. None of them mentioned the one thought that was in their heads. Water. How much longer could they last without something to drink?

The stars began to pale a little. They had come to a plateau after the steep downward climb, but they had to go on before the light was strong enough for the reconnaissance helicopters to discover them.

The night was still clear and cold. Mother and

Fatima stood out like ghostly shadows in the dark. It was so unbearably quiet that Hajdar expected any noise at all would end the spell, and he would wake up on his mattress on the floor at home. But the thirst and the split lips, the cold of the night and Mother's heavy breathing in the silence all made him realize how real it was.

When Hajdar looked ahead again, he thought he was seeing things. Was it possible? A good way in front of them was a village on the side of the mountain. Hajdar turned to Bibigoll and Fatima and pointed. When they came closer to the gray-brown clay huts, they discovered that most of them had collapsed. There wasn't a sign of any living thing.

Hajdar plucked up his courage.

"Hello! Is there anyone here?" There was no answer. They continued walking through one of the open gates into a yard. Hajdar looked more closely at the collapsed dwelling and understood at once. They had come to a village that had been bombed just like their own.

Eventually they found a hut that had escaped destruction. A little hesitantly they went in the open door. Pots and clay containers stood in a pile by the fire. There were still some moldy remnants of food in some of them. On the floor against the walls were mattresses. Bibigoll and Fatima sank down without a word.

"Rest here," said Hajdar. "I'll be back soon."

When he returned he was holding a large clay pot with water dripping from a little hole in the bottom. He had managed to find a well that was still intact.

They unrolled their blankets, and Fatima and Bibigoll fell asleep quickly. Hajdar wanted to sleep, but now, when he finally had a chance, he couldn't. Thoughts of the past several months kept going around in his head.

Late fall in the village had been a very busy time, because all the huts had to be rebuilt. They mixed clay and straw and dried bricks in the sun. Many people had to content themselves with smaller huts for the time being, but with a great deal of work, everyone had a place to sleep by winter. Many women had lost their husbands in the bomb attack. There were children with no parents. But people helped one another like never before.

The landowner had, it seemed, heard about the bombing and kept away. The Muslim priest had disappeared from the village — no one knew where. Hajdar helped the children who had just begun to learn to read. Sometimes at night guerrillas turned up asking for food so they could keep on fighting in the mountains.

The radio in Saber's home had been destroyed by the bombs, but Hajdar crept over to another neighbor's house and listened to the news at night. A new president had come — again. He had asked for help from Russia, the large country in the north, and they had sent tens of thousands of soldiers to help conquer Afghanistan's enemies.

But the resistance men who came at night told another story. Afghanistan was not a free country anymore, they said. The president had sold it to the Russians. Some other villages on the plain had also been bombed by the Russians. Their water pipelines had been destroyed, and all the village inhabitants had fled to Pakistan. There could be no harvest, no life, without water.

As Hajdar listened to these things, a thought began to take root in his mind. No one knew when their village would be bombed next. Perhaps government soldiers would come and burn the harvest as he had heard they had done in other villages.

In the spring, Hajdar helped his father's brothers to sow, but he knew he would not be there at harvest time. Fatima and Bibigoll still knew nothing of his plans, but at night he sometimes asked the guerrillas about good escape routes, and tried to memorize what he was told.

Then the last evening came. Fatima and Mother didn't want to go, but they understood that there was no alternative. Grandmother had cried when she had heard what they were planning to do. She was sure her sons would look after her, but her most loved son was gone forever, and now his son was going, too. They had not dared tell the others in the village.

While it was still dark they prepared to leave. Hajdar gave Grandmother the gray songbird. On the way out of the village they went by the graveyard one last time. Then Mother turned around and looked at the village where she had lived all her life.

"Never again," she said quietly.

Soon they were sitting on the bus to Kabul, and from there the journey continued to a town near the Pakistani border. They spent a great deal of their money buying a donkey to carry their loads for them on the mountain paths, but they soon realized that they had been tricked. They almost had to carry the donkey and were forced to leave both it and some of their things near a mountain village.

When the guerrillas had described it, the road over the border had seemed so short. But now they had been walking and walking — through heat and cold and lashing sandstorms.

Hajdar didn't know how long they had been sleeping when he heard noises outside. He was sure border guards had somehow found out that they were hiding in the house.

Suddenly five bearded men with rifles were standing in front of them. Hajdar raised himself up on his elbows.

"What are you doing here?" asked one of the men.

"We have just been sleeping. We are going toward the border."

"We had also thought about sleeping, but we are going back to Afghanistan," said the man, and his look softened. Hajdar breathed a sigh of relief.

"They are guerrillas," he told Fatima and Bibigoll. The men had slipped in from Pakistan and were going to fight the Russians for a few months before going back to their base again. They were waiting in the abandoned village to meet up with other guerrillas.

A little while later all eight of them were sharing their last bits of bread, though they didn't dare heat water for tea, because the smoke could give them away. When it began to get dark, they drank as much water as they could swallow without getting sick, and found two clay pots that they could fill with water and carry away with them.

They were just about to go when one of the men stopped them. "Watch out where you put your feet," he said. "They drop land mines from helicopters. If you tread on a mine, you're dead. And don't pick up anything from the ground. Sometimes they make land mines that look like cigarette cartons and toys. Lots of people have lost their hands and arms."

Then, after giving them a careful description of the route to take, the men disappeared into the darkness.

14

I<small>T</small> was another bright, clear night. The long rest had been good for them, and for once they were no longer thirsty.

The path descended more and more steeply. At times they had to get down on their hands and knees and crawl forward. What the guerrillas had described as a few hours' walk seemed endless. Bibigoll found it hard to keep up, and Hajdar and Fatima had to stop frequently so she could catch her breath. Their bodies were screaming for food.

"Take this," said Bibigoll suddenly as she pulled something from her pocket. In the semi-dusk it looked as though she was holding two balls. Hajdar took one ball, smelled it and held it up toward the light of the stars. Then he realized what it was.

He remembered a story his grandmother had told him about a time long ago, when the Afghans' enemies had surrounded them and shut the Afghan army off in a little valley. But the army continued to fight day after day, and the enemy couldn't understand how the people in the valley could manage for so long without food. Eventually they were forced to leave the Afghans without defeating them.

Hajdar knew he was holding the secret of the Afghan victory in his hand — dried mulberry figs and walnuts, ground and pressed for days under heavy stones. The soldiers had had lots of this compact mass hidden in their clothes. The mixture was so full of energy that just a few bites gave them the strength to fight the whole day. And Bibigoll, who thought of everything, had brought some of these balls to eat once the bread was gone.

They continued their journey all through the night. Many times Bibigoll sat down and asked them to leave her on the mountainside.

"You are young. It's better that you get there before daylight. Otherwise we'll all be shot."

They led her, dragged her and almost carried her part of the way. The stars were getting paler in the sky. Soon the sun would rise over them.

They came over yet another peak, expecting to see a new mountain in front of them. But instead, a valley spread out before their feet. The starlight was reflected in a river that divided the valley in two like a silver snake. And there on the river bank, they could see a blessed sight — hundreds of small, faint points of light.

When they approached, they discovered that the whole mountainside was full of tents. They could hear a faint call to prayer, even though they couldn't see a mosque nearby. The call echoed over the mountain.

They were soon stopped by a guard who wrote down their names and the date. If they contacted him later, he said, he would see if he could find a tent for them. Then he continued on his endless walk around the tent town.

Bibigoll cried quietly. Hajdar didn't know if it was from sadness, happiness, tiredness or all these things at once. That's what he felt. They sank down onto the ground and wrapped their blankets tightly around them.

As the sun rose, the tent town slowly came to life. They could hear the cries of children and sheep. In several places, pillars of smoke rose against the clear morning sky. They could also hear the clatter of cooking pots, and people could be seen at tent openings, pulling their clothes around them and shivering in the morning cold.

"Did you arrive last night?" They looked up and saw an old woman. Bibigoll nodded.

"Come with me!" They followed the woman between the rows of tents. How could anyone find their way among these hundreds of tents that all looked the same? The old lady stopped in front of a little open fire.

"Sit down," she said. "Tea. Freshly baked bread. Help yourselves!"

Never had bread and tea tasted so good.

A short distance away stood a boy who seemed to be some years younger than Hajdar. He stared at the bread and the tea so much that Hajdar had to look the other way.

The old lady bent down and whispered, "Poor child. He is an orphan and no one knows how he got here over the mountains. Come and eat," she shouted to the boy. As quick as a flash, he grabbed some bits of bread and disappeared.

"He gets a little food here, a little there, but no one wants him," said the woman.

After the boy had gobbled up the bread crusts, he pushed his inquisitive face out from behind the nearest tent cloth.

"No, you can't have any more," said the old woman harshly. He quickly disappeared behind the tent, but his head soon popped up again.

Hajdar stood up and walked slowly toward him. At first the boy looked as though he was going to run away.

"Hello, what's your name?" asked Hajdar.

"Abdul Hadi."

"I'm called Hajdar. Can you show me where you register?"

Abdul Hadi led them to a uniformed Pakistani man who sat at a table surrounded by people. He tried to wave them away.

"I can't help you all at once. Who has just arrived at the camp?" There was silence and everyone looked around. Hajdar waved his hands eagerly.

"We came in the night and the guard has already

written up our names," he shouted while he elbowed his way to the table. He pushed Abdul Hadi in front of him, and Fatima and Mother followed.

"Not many people came last night. Are you the one called Hajdar?" asked the official. "It says here there are three of you."

Hajdar moved to one side so the man could see Bibigoll and Fatima. "Actually, there are four of us," said Hajdar. "This is Abdul Hadi, my brother."

The first day in the refugee camp was full of new experiences. They were given food twice when they showed their registration cards. Abdul Hadi stayed close to Hajdar. He didn't say much, and Hajdar didn't want to question him until they knew each other a bit better. A little brother, he thought, and smiled contentedly.

The uniformed man at the table had said they might have to wait several weeks before they got a tent, blankets and mattresses, so Bibigoll and Fatima had to squeeze in with the old lady who had invited them for breakfast. She lived with her sister and her daughters. Hajdar and Abdul Hadi would stay in a larger tent that was used for new arrivals and guerrilla soldiers.

That night, after Abdul Hadi had fallen asleep, Hajdar went out and walked around the camp, following the light from the weak bulbs that hung on poles between the rows of tents.

He stopped and looked up at the star-filled sky.

There they were – the Plow and all the other constellations. Just like at home in the village. The mountains were as black against the night sky as the mountain ridges around Kabul. In the silence he could hear the gentle sound from the river in the valley.

He was just about to return to the large dormitory when he heard voices. Men were walking into the camp, speaking in subdued voices. Hajdar could make out their bearded faces in the half-light. Guerrillas. Their turbans shone white, and their gun barrels could be seen above their shoulders. Old furrowed faces, middle-aged men and beardless young boys – some not much older than himself. No one noticed him standing pressed against the dark tent.

Suddenly he started. Was he dreaming? With a jump he moved into the light.

"Saber!"

"Hajdar!"

They flew into each other's arms. Saber put down his gun and they sat and talked for a long time in the lamplight. Saber told Hajdar that after what had happened to Mir, he had decided to join the guerrillas. This tent town was his home, but most of the time he fought the government troops inside Afghanistan.

Hajdar didn't have to tell Saber about the night the world went to pieces. Saber knew everything but

119

didn't want to talk about it. So instead, Hajdar asked about the fighting.

"It's hard, Hajdar," Saber answered unwillingly. "But we shall never give in. We're going back in a few weeks."

They went back to the dormitory, and in the darkness Hajdar moved over and made room for Saber. On his other side he heard the regular breathing of Abdul Hadi.

Hajdar turned onto his side to sleep. He had forgotten to loosen his belt with the dagger. He felt the cold steel in his hand.

"Saber, are you asleep?"

"Mmm, almost," came a surly whisper.

"Here. Take this. I don't need it anymore." Saber held the dagger in one hand and squeezed Hajdar's arm with the other. Then he fell asleep.

From far away Hajdar heard a familiar noise, a faint tinkling. Camel bells. Nomads looking for grazing ground for their cattle. One day he would go with them. Over the mountains to a little gray-brown village on the plains. To an old woman who listened to a gray songbird. And waited for the sound of camel bells.